CAPTAIN ABDUL'S PIRATE SCHOOL

Colin McNaughton has written and illustrated many books for children, including *Have You Seen Who's Just Moved In Next Door To Us?* (Winner of the Kurt Maschler Award) and *Here Come the Aliens!* (shortlisted for the Kate Greenaway Medal), *Jolly Roger*, *Dracula's Tomb* and a collection of tales about Preston Pig. His four hugely popular poetry titles, including the hilarious collection about disastrous holidays, *Wish You Were Here (And I Wasn't)*, are all now available on audio cassette, read by Colin himself.

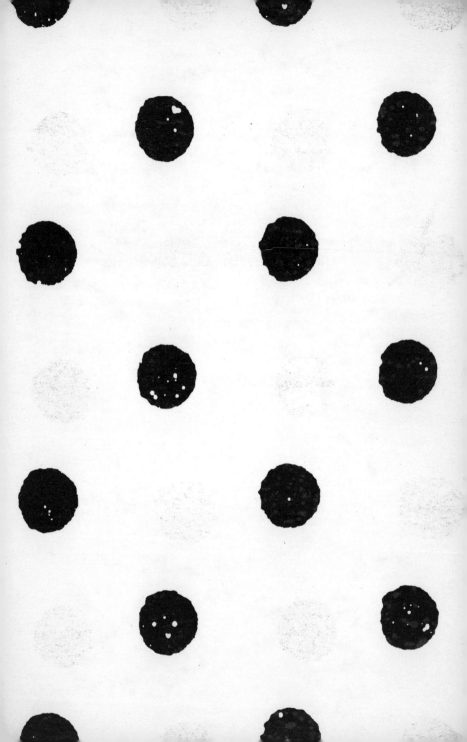

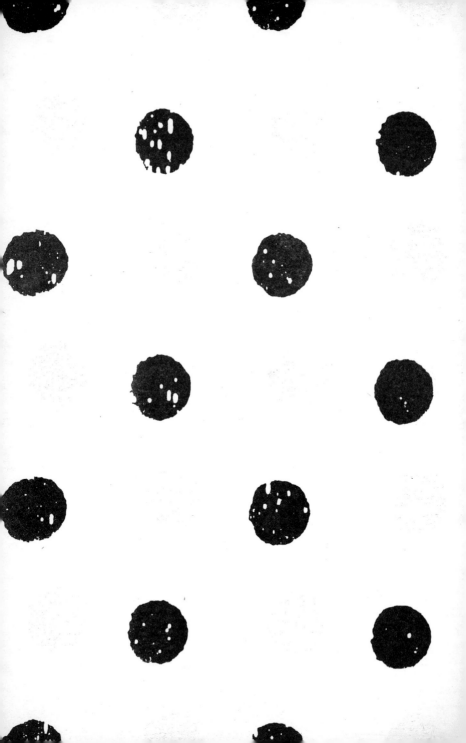

CAPTAIN ABDUL'S
PIRATE SCHOOL

For Rocky Lawson,
the first pirate I ever met

First published 1994 by Walker Books Ltd
87 Vauxhall Walk, London SE11 5HJ

Sprinters edition published 2001

This edition produced 2002 for
The Book People Ltd, Hall Wood Avenue,
Haydock, St Helens WA11 9UL

© 1994, 2001 Colin McNaughton

This book has been typeset in Garamond 3

Printed and bound in Great Britain
by The Guernsey Press Co. Ltd

British Library Cataloguing in Publication Data:
a catalogue record for this book
is available from the British Library

ISBN 0-7445-5242-7

CAPTAIN ABDUL'S
PIRATE SCHOOL

COLIN MᶜNAUGHTON

TED SMART

Dear Diary,

Well, here I stinking am! My first stinking day at Captain Abdul's Pirate School. My stinking dad has sent me here because he says I'm a big softie! (Just because I like writing poems and painting pictures!) He says it will toughen me up. He says a kid my age should jump at the chance of becoming a pirate. He says that when he was a kid he wanted to be a pirate and so should I.

He says I should be grateful.

Well, I say, "Nuts!" and I say, "Steaming cowdung!" and I say, "I hope he swallows his pipe!"

P.S. I have a secret.

I have smuggled my little dog Spud in my trunk. He's the only friend I've got in the whole stinking world!

We were met at the door by
Captain Abdul himself: hairy,
scary and with more bits missing
than a second-hand jigsaw.

"Follow me upstairs, me little buccaneers," said Captain Abdul, "an' we'll get yer kit stowed away, ooh-arrgh, that we will. Ha-har, ooh-arrgh!"

Later, Captain Abdul took us

Next we were given our school
uniforms and told to introduce
ourselves.

Jim
Silver

Françoise
du Plonk

Ching
Yih

Ali
Khoja

Unfortunately, Spud thought this included him! Luckily the captain likes dogs and said he could stay (for a small fee).

Henry Morgan

Rosemary Lavender

Pickles

Woof!

Spud

I was a bit nervous about meeting the other kids but they don't seem too bad – they look just as miserable as me.

Tom Tew

Anne Bonney

Frankie Drake

Samuel P. Chop

We then had supper and went to
bed, where I wrote this and cried
a bit for my mum.

Jack Rackam

Simon Smee

Ben Gunn

Bartholomew
Sharp

Mary Read

Beryl Flynn

Dear Diary,

Woke up this morning and stood up in bed. Forgot I was in a hammock – bit of a headache. I was brushing my teeth when Bully-boy McCoy came in.

"What yer doin' that for?" he asked.

Who ever heard of a pirate with nice teeth!

"If I don't, sir, my teeth will go black and fall out," I replied.

"What's wrong with that?" he said. "Who ever heard of a pirate with nice teeth!" And he confiscated my toothbrush!

Today we studied history.
Portobello Billy told us an exciting
story about Calico Jack the pirate,
set in his favourite place –
the West Indies.

Dear Diary,

We were queueing for breakfast this morning when Walker the Plank came over and asked Rosemary Lavender if she was pushing in.

"Yes, sir," admitted Rosemary.

"Well done!" said Walker the Plank and walked away.

Today's lessons were maths and geography. In maths we learned about angles. (You use them when aiming cannon.) In geography we learned where the West Indies are and how to read treasure maps.

Dear Diary,

The beastly Captain Abdul has scolded me for being too neat and tidy. He suspects me of brushing my hair –

"Combs an' hairbrushes, the possession of, is a floggin' offence, ooh-arrgh!" he told me.

Today we had arts and crafts. We learned how to make cannon balls, swords, fake money and how to put model ships into rum bottles. (Spanish Omar Lette very kindly emptied the bottles for us.)

Dear Diary,

Last night we were doing our homework when Riff-raff Rafferty came in and caught little Simon Smee copying from another boy.

"Was you cheatin', boy?" howled Riff-raff.

"Yes, sir," said Simon Smee in a small voice.

"Good boy!" yelled the teacher. "Go to the top of the class!"

35

Today we learned how to speak pirate. Can't wait till next week's lesson. It's pirate swearwords! Ooh-arrgh!

Dear Diary,

The teachers had a party last night!
They kept coming up and saying it
was much too early to be in bed and
why weren't we having a midnight
feast or rampaging round the town
looking for trouble!

"Why, when I was your age," said
the captain, "I already had a
wooden leg! Ooh-arrgh!"

When he finally woke up today he bellowed, "Fresh air is what we need, ooh-arrgh! We're goin' to sea!"

For the rest of the day we sailed around the harbour in the *Golden Behind*, learning pirate stuff.

Dear Diary,

Tricked! Betrayed! Duped! Fiddled! Fooled and double-crossed! Last night, after I'd taken Spud for a walk, he ran into the staffroom and I followed him in.

From the shadow of the captain's hammock, hidden by clouds of tobacco smoke, I heard terrible things…

"KIDNAP!" I yelled, when I got back to our quarters. "Captain Abdul and his dirty double-crossing teachers are going to kidnap us tonight and when our mums and dads arrive tomorrow for parents' day, all they will find will be a ransom note! We must do something!"

Arrgh!

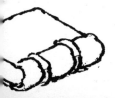

"But what?" asked
the kids.

"MUTINY!" said I.
"We get them before
they get us!"

"YES!" everyone
shouted.

"Shush!" I hissed.
"Get your swords and
follow me. Tom, you
bring the ropes."

"Aye-aye, Captain!"
said Tom. "I mean,
yes, Pickles."

Armed to the teeth with swords
and ropes, our fearless band of pirate
pupils crept down to the staffroom.

I gave the order and we attacked!

The battle was over in minutes.
We swarmed all over the pirate
teachers and tied them up with so
much rope they looked like cocoons!

We rolled the teachers out onto
the quayside.

One of the kids shouted, "What now?

"We sail for the West Indies!" I cried.
"Who's with me? Who really wants to
be a pirate?"

"ME! ME! ME!" they all shouted.

"Good!" said I. "Raid the kitchen, fill the water barrels and get the ship ready. We sail in ten minutes!"

I wrote a note to our parents telling them what had happened, pinned it to Captain Abdul and we set sail.

Dear Diary, (six months later)
This is the life! We now call
ourselves "Pirate pirates" because
we only steal from other pirates.
On our last raid we found out that
pirates from all around the world
had heard about our mutiny.

Thinking how well taught we
must have been, they have sent
their kids to Captain Abdul's
school! Abdul claims the mutiny
was all his idea – part of his
teaching plan. The scoundrel!

And so everybody is happy: Captain Abdul because his school is a roaring success and our parents because we send lots of treasure home.

The kids are happy because they get to sail and swim and fight and fire cannon and rob bullies and stay up all night!

And me? Well,
I paint my pictures
and write my poems
and I'm captain of
my own pirate ship!
Who could ask for
anything more…

I'm Captain
Maisy Pickles –
the happiest girl
in the whole, wide,
wonderful world!

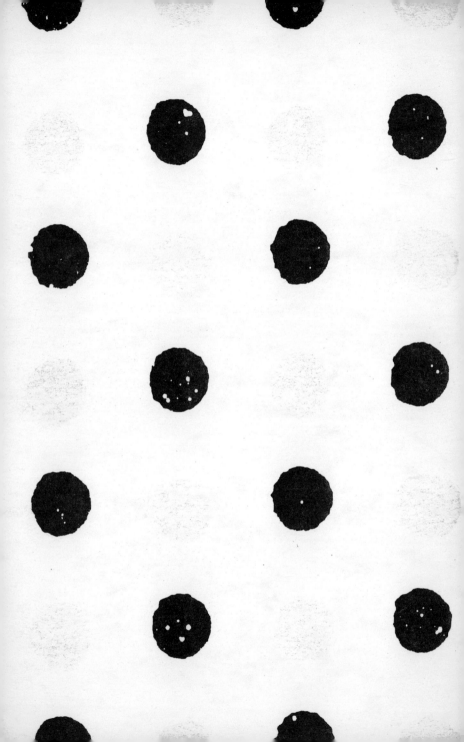

More *SPRINTERS* for you to enjoy!

- *Little Stupendo Flies High* Jon Blake   0-7445-5970-7

- *Captain Abdul's Pirate School* Colin McNaughton   0-7445-5242-7

- *The Ghost in Annie's Room* Philippa Pearce   0-7445-5993-6

- *Molly and the Beanstalk* Pippa Goodhart   0-7445-5981-2

- *Taking the Cat's Way Home* Jan Mark   0-7445-8268-7

- *The Finger-eater* Dick King-Smith   0-7445-8269-5

- *Care of Henry* Anne Fine   0-7445-8270-9

- *The Impossible Parents Go Green* Brian Patten   0-7445-7881-7

- *Flora's Fantastic Revenge* Nick Warburton   0-7445-7898-1

- *Jolly Roger* Colin McNaughton   0-7445-8293-8

- *The Haunting of Pip Parker* Anne Fine   0-7445-8294-6

- *Tarquin the Wonder Horse* June Crebbin   0-7445-7882-5

All at £3.99

LADY LONG-LEGS

Nisba may be new at her school, but she's not going to let the older girls push her around!

Jan Mark is one of the most distinguished authors of books for young people. She has twice been awarded the Carnegie Medal and has also won the Penguin Guardian Award, the Observer Teenage Fiction Prize and the Angel Award for Fiction. Her many titles for Walker Books include *The Snow Maze* and *Taking the Cat's Way Home* as well as the picture books *Fur, Strat and Chatto* (Winner of the 1990 Mother Goose Award), *This Bowl of Earth, The Tale of Tobias* and *The Midas Touch*. Jan Mark lives in Oxford.

"An immensely satisfying story … demonstrates the very best in writing for developing readers."
The Sunday Telegraph

JAN MARK

LADY LONG-LEGS

Illustrations by Paul Howard

TED SMART

For Nisba, Neesa and Aishe

First published 1999 by
Walker Books Ltd, 87 Vauxhall Walk
London SE11 5HJ

This edition published 2001

2 4 6 8 10 9 7 5 3 1

Text © 1999 Jan Mark
Illustrations © 1999, 2001 Paul Howard

This book has been typeset in Garamond

Printed and bound in Great Britain
by The Guernsey Press Co. Ltd

British Library Cataloguing in Publication Data:
a catalogue record for this book is
available from the British Library

ISBN 0-7445-8296-2

Contents

Chapter One

Nisba was a new girl. Everyone else in her class had been at Farm Lane School for three years and one term. Nisba had been there for three days.

It was cold and frosty outside, but the hall was warm and cosy.

After assembly, Nisba said to Mr Martin, "Where does the warm come from?"

"Warmth," Mr Martin said. "Do you know what, Nisba? You are the first person who has ever asked me that."

Mr Martin liked people to ask him questions. He was not so happy when they told him things. They told him things all day long.

"Sir, Neesa's got mud on her shoes."

"Mr Martin, Aishe's taken my crayons."

"Farid's hitting Robert, Sir."

Nisba was new. She had nothing to tell him yet.

"We have under-floor heating," Mr Martin said. "There are hot pipes down there under the floor tiles. That is why the tiles keep coming unstuck. The glue melts and the tiles split."

The floor of the hall was red and black tiles, but in places there were blue tiles instead of black ones, and pink tiles instead of red ones. Mr Keates, the caretaker, never had enough of the right colours when he mended the floor.

And there was one white tile, almost in the middle of the doorway. Nisba had learned one important thing already. It was very bad luck to walk on the white tile. If someone walked on the white tile they had to stand on one leg and count to twenty, with their fingers crossed. Otherwise they got bad luck.

On the very first day Robert had fallen down the steps in the corridor and broken his arm. Everyone said it was because he walked on the white tile going in to assembly and didn't bother to count to twenty with his fingers crossed.

Robert said it was because Farid had pushed him, but everyone knew about the white tile. Aishe had seen him walk on it.

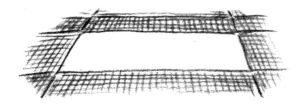

Chapter Two

Nisba was not afraid of the white tile in the hall, so she walked on it. People said that if you stood on a blue tile and a pink tile at the same time, all your teeth would fall out. No one dared to try it.

Mr Keates did it all the time. He had false teeth.

It was different in the corridor. In the corridor the tiles were brown.

"Brown is the colour of footprints," Mr Martin said. "The colour of mud and dust and old, old dinner."

But not all of the tiles were brown. Down the middle of the corridor there was a pattern like a hopscotch grid, made of green and yellow tiles.

17

They were not allowed to play
hopscotch indoors but the patterns
were not wasted. Some people
would walk only on brown tiles.

Some people took big steps and
walked only on yellow tiles. The
ones with very long legs could get
all the way from the front door to
the hall on green tiles.

The six steps by the staff room
were all brown. They did not count.

Nisba had long legs. On the fourth day of term she went right down the corridor on green tiles, but as she passed the cloakroom a big girl came out. It was Lucy Wells.

"You can't do that," Lucy said. "It's not allowed."

"What isn't?" Nisba said.

"Only people in Year 4 can walk on green tiles," Lucy said.

Nisba looked at Lucy. "What year are you in?"

"Year 4," Lucy said. "You're not in Year 4."

Nisba took a big step from one green tile to the next.

Lucy stamped. "You can't do that!"

"Yes I can," Nisba said, and took another step.

Lucy gave her a hard push.

"If I see you walking on green tiles again, you'll be in trouble."

Mrs Higgins came along. She was the Head Teacher.

"You ought to be in your classrooms now," she said. "Hurry up."

Lucy went into the Year 4 room. As she opened the door she turned round and gave Nisba a nasty look.

"Stay off those green tiles," Lucy said. "Daddy-long-legs."

Chapter Three

"I've got another question," Nisba said to Mr Martin. "Why can't Year 3 people walk on the green tiles?"

"I don't know," Mr Martin said. "Tell me about it."

Nisba did not want to tell tales.

"In the corridor," she said. "There are lots of brown tiles and some yellow tiles and not many green tiles. Someone said only Year 4 people can walk on the green tiles."

"Ah, I see," said Mr Martin. "Well, once upon a time, people used to play hopscotch on the yellow and green tiles, and there were accidents, so the rule is, no jumping. But Year 4 people are taller. They can take bigger steps. There's no rule about that."

"I can take bigger steps too,"
Nisba said.

Mr Martin looked at her.

"You're a very tall girl, Nisba," he
said. "You go ahead and walk
where you like."

At lunch-time, Nisba went up the corridor on the green tiles, and into the cloakroom.

Lucy Wells was waiting for her.

"I saw you walking on the green tiles," Lucy said. She had friends with her.

"Mr Martin said I could walk on them," Nisba said. "Mr Martin says I can walk where I like."

"It's nothing to do with him," said one of Lucy's friends. "We say you can't."

"Anyway," Lucy said, "you're a new girl. New girls can only walk on brown tiles. Everyone knows that."

Nisba looked at Lucy and Lucy's friends. None of them was as tall as Nisba. Suddenly she understood. They were angry because she *could* reach the green tiles without jumping, not because she *did*.

Silly little things, Nisba thought. She went out of the cloakroom and stood on a green tile. Someone behind her hooked a foot round her ankle. She lost her balance and fell over, hitting her arm on the step at the bottom of the staircase.

Chapter Four

Mrs Higgins came out of the staff room and saw Nisba sitting on the floor. Nisba was trying not to cry. Lucy was pretending that she had just come out of the cloakroom. Lucy's friends began to look at a picture on the wall.

"Lucy and Nisba *again*?" Mrs Higgins said. "I hope you're not fighting."

"I slipped on the tiles," Nisba said.

"Yes, she slipped," said Lucy, and Lucy's friends.

Nisba stood up. She had a big red mark on her arm.

"That will be a nasty bruise," Mrs Higgins said. "You need the Hand of Peace on that. Go to the staff room and say I sent you. The rest of you get your lunch."

Nisba went up the steps to the staff room and knocked on the door.

Miss Shah came out. "Who are you?" she said.

"I'm Nisba," Nisba said. "I'm new. Mrs Higgins says I need the Hand of Peace."

She showed Miss Shah her bruise.

"Come in, then," Miss Shah said. "How did you do that?"

"I slipped and fell on the steps," Nisba said. She followed Miss Shah into the staff room.

All the teachers were sitting in comfy chairs, eating their lunch and drinking coffee. In the corner was a sink, and a draining board, and a little fridge.

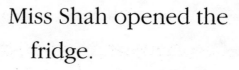

Miss Shah opened the fridge.

"Will it hurt?" Nisba said, as Miss Shah took something out of the ice box.

"You tell me," Miss Shah said. "It looks as if it hurts already."

"No, not my arm. The Hand of Peace."

Miss Shah laughed. "It's not the Hand of *Peace*, Nisba, it's the Hand of *Peas*. Someone found out that a good thing for a bruise is to put a packet of frozen peas on it. We've got something even better."

She was holding a white plastic glove, tied at the wrist with string.

"The peas are in the glove," Miss Shah said. "Go and sit in the front hall for a bit. Hold the glove against your poor arm and it will feel like a nice cool hand."

Chapter Five

The front hall was a good place to
sit. There were armchairs for
visitors, and a piece of carpet, and
three tall plants in pots.

Nisba had sat here once before,
with Mum, when they came to ask
Mrs Higgins if Nisba could go to
Farm Lane School.

Nisba took the best chair and held
the Hand of Peas against her bruise.
It was so cold she could feel it
making the swelling go down. It felt
like peace, even if it was only
frozen peas.

From her chair Nisba could see past the staff room, down the steps and along the corridor.

Mrs Higgins was there, with Mr Keates the caretaker. They were crawling about, poking the floor.

Mrs Higgins did not often crawl about on the floor. She had nice trousers on, too.

"Here's another," Mr Keates said. "Split right across. It's those pipes again."

"One of the little ones tripped just now," Mrs Higgins said.

That's me, Nisba thought. They think I tripped on a loose tile. But I'm not little. That's the trouble.

Mrs Higgins came back up the steps and saw Nisba.

"Better now?" she said.

"Yes, thank you," Nisba said.

"Go and have your lunch, then," Mrs Higgins said. She went into her special room with HEAD TEACHER on the door.

Nisba took the Hand of Peas off her arm. Now her skin was icy cold and the Hand was warm and floppy. She knocked on the door of the staff room. Miss Shah came to take the Hand away.

"I'll put it back in the fridge to get cold for someone else," she said.

Nisba walked down the steps and along the corridor. Now that she was looking for them she could see the split tiles. Some of the green tiles were split, but she stepped on them anyway, because Lucy had said she must not.

She did not really want to walk on green tiles all the time, but Lucy was a bully, and bullies must never be allowed to win.

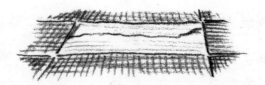

Chapter Six

Then it was Saturday. There was no school for two whole days, so Nisba wore her bangles. But every time she looked at her arm she saw the fading bruise, and thought of Lucy.

Was Lucy a bully? Bullies were supposed to be big and tough. Nisba was bigger than Lucy, but Lucy had friends.

Four little bullies were as bad as one big one.

On Monday it was very cold. As Nisba walked across the playground she thought of the warm floor in the hall where they would sit for assembly.

She hung up her coat in the cloakroom and went into the corridor. Something had happened. Something was different.

It was the floor.

During the weekend Mr Keates had been at work. Nisba remembered how he had crawled on the floor with Mrs Higgins, counting split tiles. He had taken them all away and put new ones down.

The new tiles were grey, and they were all over the place. Some of them were in the hopscotch patterns instead of green tiles or yellow ones. No one could walk down the corridor on only green tiles now, they were too far apart.

Not even Mr Martin would be able to do it, and he was the tallest teacher.

At the end of the corridor by the Year 4 room, people were trying to walk on green tiles. Lucy took a huge step but it was no use, she could not reach.

"Nyah, nyah," Lucy said, when she saw Nisba. "Now you'll have to walk on the brown tiles, Daddy-long-legs."

"No I won't," Nisba said, and she walked all the way down the corridor on the new grey tiles. It was the hardest thing she had ever done and she nearly fell over twice, but she stepped on every grey tile.

Lucy and her friends were growling.

When Nisba got to the end of the corridor they all started to walk the other way, but no one else could step on all the grey tiles. They had to hop between some of them.

Neesa and Aishe were watching. They went into the Year 3 room and fetched Mr Martin. They knew what Lucy was like. They knew what Lucy had done to Nisba.

"People are jumping in the corridor," Neesa said. "They mustn't do that, must they?"

"No," said Mr Martin, and he came out to see what was going on.

Chapter Seven

"Here comes Mr Martin. Look out!"
said one of Lucy's friends.

Lucy was just starting to jump. She
tried to stop but it was too late, and
she sat down hard on the floor.

"What's all this?" Mr Martin said.
Lucy started to cry.

"Have you hurt yourself?" Mr
Martin said.

"I bumped my head," Lucy said.
It was not true. She had bumped
her bottom but she did not want to
say so.

"Go and get the Hand of Peas,"
Mr Martin said. "If we have any more
accidents they will close the school.
Now, what are you all doing?"

No one said anything.

"I hear you have been jumping,"
Mr Martin said. "Were you playing
hopscotch? You know that is not
allowed."

"I was walking on the grey tiles," Nisba said. "I wasn't jumping."

Lucy came back. She had the Hand of Peas on her head. "I didn't jump," she said. "Not really, I didn't. I just didn't quite walk."

"And I can't quite fly," Mr Martin said. "Jumping is both feet off the ground at once. I know all about how you walk on special tiles, but walking is not jumping. Let's see who can do it. Start at the steps and see how far you get."

One after the other the Year 4
people tried to walk down the
corridor, stepping only on the new
grey tiles, but no one could do it.

"Now Nisba," Mr Martin said, and Nisba went down the corridor again, stepping on the grey tiles.

"That's not fair," Lucy said. "She's only got a little bit of her foot on some of those tiles."

"It is fair," Aishe said. "Robert only had a tiny bit of his foot on the white tile, but he still broke his arm."

"This could get dangerous," Mr Martin said. "What have you started, Nisba?"

"I'm sorry," Nisba said, but she did not think she had done anything wrong.

"You need not be sorry," Mr Martin said, "but are you always going to walk on the grey tiles?"

"No," Nisba said. "It hurts my legs where they join on. I just wanted to see if I could."

57

"There," Mr Martin said. "Do you understand? You don't *have* to do something just because you *can*. If Nisba stops walking on the grey tiles, will the rest of you stop trying to?"

They all nodded, but Lucy hissed, "Daddy-long-legs."

"Stop it, Lucy," Mr Martin said. "And do put that horrible Hand back in the fridge. It looks as if someone is trying to pull your head off."

"Nisba can't be a daddy," Neesa said. "She's a girl."

"She'll be a lady, not a daddy," Aishe said.

And Nisba said, "That's right. I'm Lady Long-legs."

More SPRINTERS for you to enjoy!

- *Little Stupendo Flies High* Jon Blake   0-7445-5970-7

- *Captain Abdul's Pirate School* Colin McNaughton 0-7445-5242-7

- *The Ghost in Annie's Room* Philippa Pearce   0-7445-5993-6

- *Molly and the Beanstalk* Pippa Goodhart   0-7445-5981-2

- *Taking the Cat's Way Home* Jan Mark   0-7445-8268-7

- *The Finger-eater* Dick King-Smith   0-7445-8269-5

- *Care of Henry* Anne Fine   0-7445-8270-9

- *The Impossible Parents Go Green* Brian Patten   0-7445-7881-7

- *Flora's Fantastic Revenge* Nick Warburton   0-7445-7898-1

- *Jolly Roger* Colin McNaughton   0-7445-8293-8

- *The Haunting of Pip Parker* Anne Fine   0-7445-8294-6

- *Tarquin the Wonder Horse* June Crebbin   0-7445-7882-5

- *Cup Final Kid* Martin Waddell   0-7445-8297-0

- *Lady Long-legs* Jan Mark   0-7445-8296-2

- *Ronnie and the Giant Millipede* Jenny Nimmo   0-7445-8298-9

All at £3.99

CARE OF HENRY

When Hugo's mother goes into hospital, he must decide who he wants to stay with. The key to it all is Henry, his dog.

Anne Fine was elected to take on the prestigious position of Children's Laureate in 2001. A highly acclaimed author, she has won the Smarties Book Prize, the Guardian Children's Fiction Award and, on two occasions, the Carnegie Medal and the Whitbread Children's Book Award, most recently for *The Tulip Touch*. She was also voted Children's Author of the Year in 1990 and 1993. Her book *Goggle-eyes* was dramatized as a BBC TV serial and *Madame Doubtfire* was turned into the hugely successful Hollywood film, *Mrs Doubtfire*. She has two daughters and lives in County Durham.

You can find out more about Anne Fine and her books by visiting her website: www.annefine.co.uk

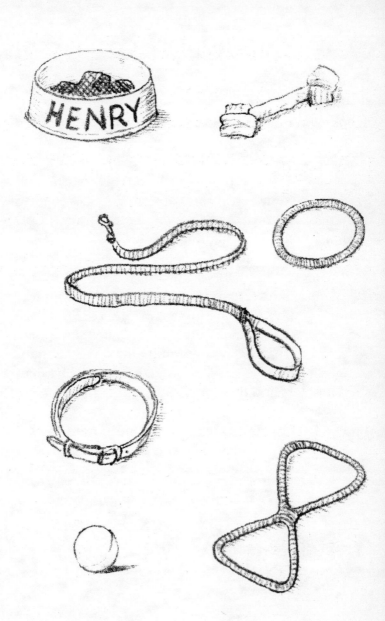

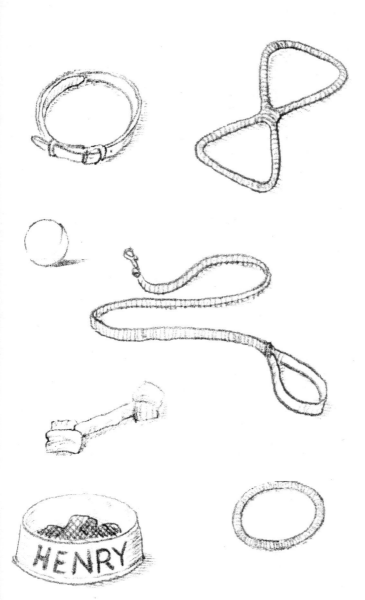

ANNE FINE

Illustrations by Paul Howard

TED SMART

For Annie
P.H.

First published 1996 by
Walker Books Ltd, 87 Vauxhall Walk
London SE11 5HJ

This edition produced 2002 for
The Book People Ltd, Hall Wood Avenue,
Haydock, St Helens WA11 9UL

2 4 6 8 10 9 7 5 3 1

Text © 1996 Anne Fine
Illustrations © 1996 Paul Howard

The right of Anne Fine to be identified as author of this
work has been asserted by her in accordance with the
Copyright, Designs and Patents Act 1988

This book has been typeset in Garamond

Printed and bound in Great Britain by The Guernsey Press Co. Ltd

British Library Cataloguing in Publication Data:
a catalogue record for this book is
available from the British Library

ISBN 0-7445-8270-9

CONTENTS

Hugo's mother was going to have a baby. Very soon. She kept saying to Hugo, "I'll only be gone for three days. I'm not asking you to choose a new *mother*. Just who you're going to stay with till I get back. So, come along, Hugo. Where's it going to be? Granny's house?"

Hugo just shrugged.

"Next door with
Mrs Mariposa?"
Hugo's face
went blank.

"At Uncle Jack's flat?"
Hugo said nothing.

"How about at a posh five-star hotel, with a telly in the bedroom, and a swimming pool and a jacuzzi, all by yourself?"

"That would be lovely," said Hugo.

"I was joking," said his mother. And she waddled off to take the sheets off the line before it rained.

Hugo sat glumly stroking Henry's
ears, trying to decide. He knew he
was good at choosing some things,
like food, and what to watch on
telly. And he was bad at choosing
others. This was obviously one of
the others.

Just then, the door bell rang.

"That will be someone to look at the house," said Mum. "I hope they buy it."

"So do I," said Hugo (though he didn't look forward to helping to choose the next house).

"Fingers crossed, then," said his mother. And she answered the door.

On the step was a man with a clipboard and a pencil.

"Nice freshly painted front door," he said, and made a little mark on the paper on his clipboard.

He stepped inside.

"Fine airy hall," he said, and marked his paper again.

Hugo and Henry showed him round the house. In every room, he stood and looked, and then marked his paper. Hugo and Henry watched him.

"What are you writing?" asked Hugo. "Is it ticks and crosses for good and bad, like in school?"

The man looked a bit embarrassed. "And blanks," he said. "If it's nothing special, I just leave a blank."

"How are we doing?" asked Hugo.

The man held the clipboard to his chest, so Hugo couldn't see it. "Fine," he said heartily. "Just fine."

Hugo was interested. "So, if you put all ticks, you might buy the house?"

"I might."

"But if it was all crosses, you wouldn't?"

"No, I certainly wouldn't."

"Clever," said Hugo. "Very, very clever."

They went into the garden. The man helped Hugo's mother fold the two big sheets. And then he said goodbye.

At the gate, he tripped over
Henry and dropped the paper.
Hugo picked it up.

"There are blanks on it," Hugo
said to him. "And some crosses.
Tell me exactly what was wrong,
because Mum will want to know."

The man gazed up at the sky. Hugo guessed he was trying to think of something to say that wouldn't upset a lady who was going to have a baby any minute. In the end he said, "I think maybe some of the cupboards were a little too spacious."

Hugo went back to his mother.

"He won't buy it," he told her. "He's looking for something with a little less cupboard space."

Hugo's mother stared at the man's back as he walked away. Then she clutched her stomach suddenly.

"You're going to have to hurry up and decide," she told Hugo. "This baby won't wait much longer. Neither will I."

"All right," said Hugo testily. "Don't rush me. Don't rush me."

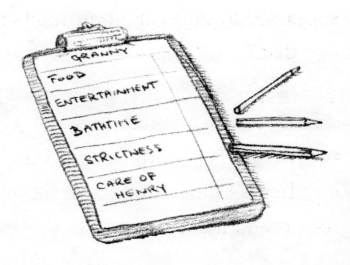

CHAPTER 2

Hugo phoned his granny. He put
his new clipboard on the table first,
and made sure he had three pencils,
in case two broke.

Then he punched the number.

Granny answered. "Hello. This is
six, four, six, six, seven, seven."

"You shouldn't say that," Hugo told her sternly. "You're not supposed to give out your number like that."

"I've always thought that was ridiculous," his granny said. "If people didn't already know your number, they couldn't have phoned you, could they?"

Hugo decided to start all over again. "Is that you, Granny?"

"Yes. Is that you, Hugo?"

"Yes, it is."

"How nice to hear from you."

"I had one or two questions," said Hugo, looking at his clipboard.

"Fire away," said his granny.

"If," Hugo said, and then he said it again, even more clearly, in case there should be any doubt, "*if* I came to sleep over at your house when Mummy goes into hospital, what will you feed me?"

He held his pencil over the first space on his sheet of paper, and waited.

The answer took a bit of time to come. Then: "Semolina," said Granny rather frostily. "I expect I should feed you semolina."

"You don't usually feed me semolina," Hugo said, putting a big black cross in Granny's FOOD space.

"You don't usually phone up and check on the menu," Granny said tartly.

"Sorry," said Hugo. "Am I being rude?"

"A little."

Hugo had a think. But he had made his chart, and it had taken him hours. He wasn't going to toss the whole thing over. He thought he'd just press on.

"What about telly?" he asked. "Would you let me watch all my favourite telly shows?"

"Not if they're at the same time as mine."

"Which are your favourites, then?" Hugo asked hopefully.

"*Songs of Praise*," said his granny. "*A Week in Politics. Antiques Roadshow.* And that splendid new documentary on the history of shipbuilding."

Hugo gave Granny a huge black cross for ENTERTAINMENT.

"What about bathtime?
Can I have it deep?"
"We're on a
water shortage,"
said Granny.
"Five inches
maximum, I'm
afraid."
"With bubbles?"
"We're clean out
of bubbles in this
house," Granny said
cheerfully.

Hugo gave her a cross
for BATHTIME and went on to the
next question. "What about school
the next day?"

26

"What about it?"

"Will you let me skip it because Mum's having a baby?"

"No," said Granny.

So Granny got a cross for STRICTNESS too.

Hugo came to the last question. "What about Henry? Can he come?"

"Of course he can come," said
Granny. "He's your dog."

"What will you feed him?"

"Rich meat and potato casserole,"
said Granny. "With wine if he likes
it that way. And leftover chocolate
pudding from the day before. And,
of course, some of your semolina, if
he's still got room."

"And can he sleep on my bed? In case things seem strange away from home for three whole days?"

"Yes. Henry can sleep on your bed," said Granny. "If you come."

"*If* I come," Hugo repeated. Then he said goodbye, and looked at Granny's score. If she were a house, he certainly wouldn't buy her. She had four huge black crosses, no blanks, and her only tick was under CARE OF HENRY.

GRANNY

FOOD	X
ENTERTAINMENT	X
BATHTIME	X
STRICTNESS	X
CARE OF HENRY	✓

Hugo sighed.

CHAPTER 3

Hugo went next door with his
clipboard to see Mrs Mariposa.
She was washing the floor, with
the twins crawling after her on all
fours. Behind the twins came the
dog. Behind the dog, the cat.

The gerbils were busy spinning their rusty wheel. The washing machine was groaning. And, on the radio, a man was singing *Nessun dorma*.

"*Nes-sun dor-ma,*" sang Mrs Mariposa. "*Nes-sun dor-ma* tonight!"

Hugo coughed loudly, but she didn't hear. He coughed again. Mrs Mariposa turned round.

"Ah, Yugo!" she sang, twirling round her mop.

Hugo put his foot on it.

"Could I ask you a couple of questions?" he began.

Mrs Mariposa hurled the mop into the corner and took Hugo on her knee. The twins and the dog fought for a place on Hugo's lap. The cat jumped on his shoulder. And Hugo had to lift up his clipboard.

"If I come over when Mum goes into hospital…"

Mrs Mariposa leaped to her feet,
spilling everyone on to the floor.

"Your mother! She is ready to go?"

"No, no," said Hugo. "I'm just
planning."

Mrs Mariposa sat down again.
"Very well," she said. "Plan away,
Yugo."

So Hugo went through the questions on his clipboard. "What will we eat?"

Mrs Mariposa threw her hands up in the air. "Ice-cream! My own special chocolate cake! We will have cherries. Yes! We will have cherries. And pizza. We will have pizza."

She looked horribly worried suddenly. "Yugo," she said. "You do *like* my pizza?"

"Oh, yes," said Hugo. "I love your pizza. I've always loved your pizza."

He gave her a giant tick for FOOD, and went on to the next question. "What about television? What will we watch?"

Mrs Mariposa shrugged. "Broken," she said. "Dead broken. But we never watch it anyway."

It was true. In all the hundreds of times Hugo had been in the house, he'd never seen anyone except the gerbils watching telly. So he gave her a blank for ENTERTAINMENT.

"What about bathtime? Can I have it deep?"

"Deep!" cried Mrs Mariposa. "You will have a bath so deep you need waterwings and a life-guard!"

The twins grabbed at Hugo as if to drag him off right now to have a bath.

"With bubbles?" asked Hugo.

"So many bubbles we won't be able to see you!"

Hugo gave her a tick. "What about strictness?"

Mrs Mariposa put out her hand, lifted his chin, and stared into his eyes. "Yugo," she said, "while you are my guest, my house is your house.

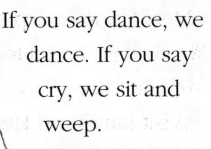

If you say dance, we dance. If you say cry, we sit and weep.

If you say…"

"That's fine," said Hugo, and he gave her a tick.

She had three big ticks already, but he carried on to the end.

"And what about care of Henry?"

"Henry?"

"Yes," Hugo said. "Henry."

Mrs Mariposa

FOOD	✓
ENTERTAINMENT	
BATHTIME	✓
STRICTNESS	✓
CARE OF HENRY	✗

Mrs Mariposa clapped her hands. "We shall go round to visit Henry every half hour."

"Visit him?" said Hugo. "Can't he come?"

Mrs Mariposa looked around, waving her hands to take in the dog, the cat, the gerbils and the twins. "Remember how it was last time Henry came?"

Hugo remembered. It had taken a full twenty minutes to pick up the broken china and sweep up the fur.

Sadly, he put a big cross under CARE OF HENRY. "Never mind," he told Mrs Mariposa. "It's your only one."

CHAPTER 4

Hugo asked Uncle Jack, "Have you got a pencil?"

Uncle Jack offered him a very flash pen.

"I have a few questions," said Hugo.

"Is it a quiz?" asked Uncle Jack. "I love a good quiz. I'm very good at..."

"Uncle Jack!" Hugo said. "If I come round when Mum goes into hospital, what will we eat?"

"Whatever we fancy," said Uncle Jack. "I don't plan ahead, like you do. If you feel like baked spuds, then that's what we'll have, if I've got any. If you're after something more special, if it's in my book, I'll cook it for you."

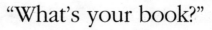

"What's your book?"
*"Fast Food For
After The Pub,"*
said Uncle Jack.
Hugo gave
Uncle Jack a
very faint and
wobbly tick for
FOOD. "Telly?"
he asked.

"Whatever you
like, Hugo. I only
watch the sport. I'll
move it into your
bedroom if you like."

Hugo gave him a big tick for
ENTERTAINMENT.

"Bathtime? Can I have it deep?"

"Deep as you like. And you can use up all that silly bubble stuff your mother gave me for Christmas."

"*All* of it?"

"All of it," said Uncle Jack firmly, earning another tick.

"What about strictness?"

"Strictness?"

"I mean, will you make me go to school the next day, and all that?"

Uncle Jack stared. "School? What? Get up early and drive you all the way over town just to go to school? You must be mad. It isn't every day your mother has a baby. No, we'll go fishing."

That was one more tick. "And what about Henry?"

"I'll phone the kennels now, to book a place."

Hugo was horrified.

"Kennels? Put Henry in a kennel for days and days?"

"What else can we do?" asked Uncle Jack. "No pets allowed in my flat."

So CARE OF HENRY was his first big cross. And it was such a big one it used up the last of the ink in Uncle Jack's flash pen.

CHAPTER 5

Hugo sat on the doorstep beside
Henry. He ran his finger over the
sheet of paper on the clipboard.

"Granny has four crosses and one
tick," he said. "Mrs Mariposa has
three ticks, one blank and one
cross. And Uncle Jack has four ticks.

46

But Mum says the *Fast Food For After The Pub* book is shocking, and the faint wobbly tick should be at least a blank, if not a cross."

He sighed. "That means I should choose Uncle Jack or Mrs Mariposa. It all depends on which I really care about – food or telly."

Henry looked mournful.

"Or you," said Hugo. "If I really care about you, then I should go to Granny's. She's the only one who has a tick under CARE OF HENRY."

They both looked mournful together. Then Hugo said glumly, "Semolina. *A Week in Politics*. Baths five centimetres deep. No bubbles. And school the next day."

He sighed again. "But," he told Henry, "you'll be able to come with me, and you can sleep on my bed."

Henry looked a little more hopeful.

"Have you decided yet?" Hugo's mother asked.

"No," said Hugo. "The ticks on the clipboard say Mrs Mariposa or Uncle Jack. But my heart says Granny."

"Go with your heart," said Mum.

Hugo took hold of Henry by the collar and looked deep into his eyes. "I hope you know I'm doing this for you," he said. "When you're gobbling your rich meat and potato casserole and leftover chocolate pudding, I hope you remember I'm eating semolina for you."

Henry gazed back at him, lovingly.

"And when I'm sitting in my dry bath, and when I'm watching *Songs of Praise*, and when I'm stuck in school, I hope you'll be grateful."

Henry blinked gratefully.

"Very well," Hugo said to his mother. "Granny's it is."

CHAPTER 6

And it wasn't at all bad, really. It
turned out that somehow Granny
had got mixed up, and made a
casserole for Hugo instead of for
Henry. (Henry made do with
dogfood.)

The leftover chocolate pudding wasn't leftover enough to give to a dog, so Hugo ate that as well. (Henry had a bone.) And there was no semolina.

"Clean out of semolina at the shop," Granny said cheerfully. "But they had plenty of bubble bath."

So Hugo had that. He ran the first few centimetres, then Granny came in and told him he could have all her inches for next week. (That took him up to the overflow.) He stayed in so long, building bubble towers, that he missed *Songs of Praise* and *Antiques Roadshow*.

He went to bed, and Henry slept
with him.

Next day Hugo visited Mum in
hospital. (*After* school.)

And the next day.

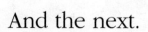
And the next.

On the day Mum was coming home, the lady waiting for Mum's bed bumped into Hugo in the corridor. Beside her was the man who came to look at Hugo's house.

"I tried your idea with the clipboard," Hugo told him.

"Did it work?"

"It might have worked," said Hugo. "I won't ever know. Because, in the end, I gave up on ticks and crosses and followed my heart."

"I expect that's the best thing to do," the man said. "I'm having a problem with all the ticks and crosses myself. Maybe I should follow my heart too."

Maybe he did. We'll never know. He didn't buy Hugo's house, anyway.

Hugo's still waiting, and his
sister's *two*.

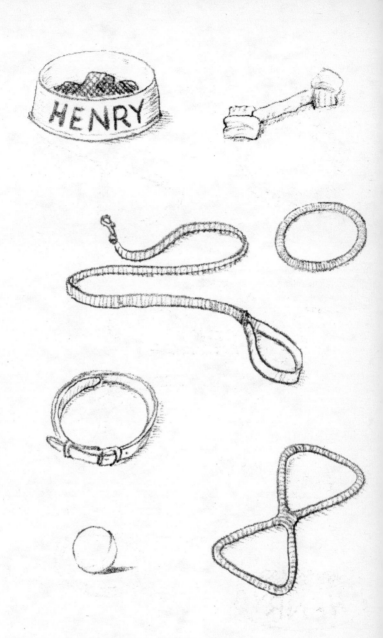

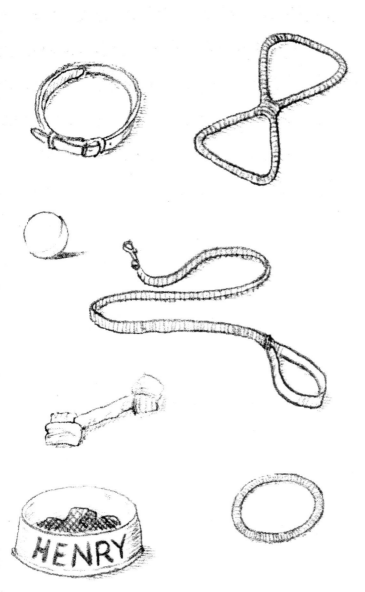

More $\mathscr{SPRINTERS}$ for you to enjoy!

- *Little Stupendo Flies High* Jon Blake   0-7445-5970-7

- *Captain Abdul's Pirate School* Colin McNaughton 0-7445-5242-7

- *The Ghost in Annie's Room* Philippa Pearce   0-7445-5993-6

- *Molly and the Beanstalk* Pippa Goodhart   0-7445-5981-2

- *Taking the Cat's Way Home* Jan Mark   0-7445-8268-7

- *The Finger-eater* Dick King-Smith   0-7445-8269-5

- *Care of Henry* Anne Fine   0-7445-8270-9

- *The Impossible Parents Go Green* Brian Patten   0-7445-7881-7

- *Flora's Fantastic Revenge* Nick Warburton   0-7445-7898-1

- *Jolly Roger* Colin McNaughton   0-7445-8293-8

- *The Haunting of Pip Parker* Anne Fine   0-7445-8294-6

- *Tarquin the Wonder Horse* June Crebbin   0-7445-7882-5

All at £3.99

RONNIE AND THE GIANT MILLIPEDE

Ronnie's banging and crashing is in danger of being stamped out!

Jenny Nimmo worked at the BBC for a number of years, ending in a spell as a director/adaptor for *Jackanory*. Her many books for young people include the Walker titles *The Stone Mouse* (Highly Commended for the Carnegie Medal), *The Owl-tree*, Winner of the 1997 Smarties Prize Gold Medal, *Toby in the Dark* and *Dog Star*. Her well-known trilogy, comprising *The Snow Spider* (Winner of the 1986 Smarties Book Prize), *Emlyn's Moon* and *The Chestnut Soldier*, has been made into a TV series. Jenny's latest title for Walker is *Tom and the Pterosaur*. She lives in a converted watermill in Wales with her artist husband and, occasionally, her three grown-up children.

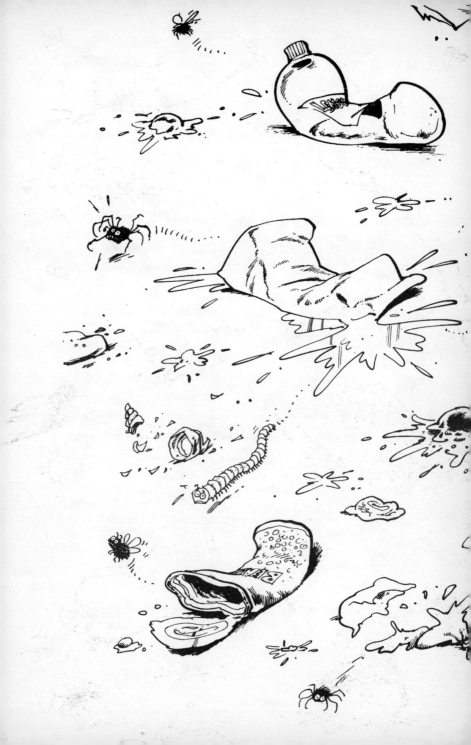

Books by the same author

The Chestnut Soldier
Dog Star
Emlyn's Moon
The Owl-tree
The Snow Spider
The Stone Mouse
Toby in the Dark
Tom and the Pterosaur

JENNY NIMMO

Illustrations by David Parkins

TED SMART

First published 1995 by
Walker Books Ltd, 87 Vauxhall Walk
London SE11 5HJ

This edition produced 2002 for
The Book People Ltd, Hall Wood Avenue,
Haydock, St Helens WA11 9UL

2 4 6 8 10 9 7 5 3 1

Text © 1995 Jenny Nimmo
Illustrations © 1995, 2001 David Parkins

This book has been typeset in Garamond

Printed and bound in Great Britain by The Guernsey Press Co. Ltd

British Library Cataloguing in Publication Data:
a catalogue record for this book is
available from the British Library

ISBN 0-7445-8298-9

CONTENTS

THE STAMPING
BEGINS

HAPPY BIRTHDAY RONNIE x

Ronnie Stiltskin was given a new
pair of boots for his seventh
birthday. They were black with
thick, heavy soles and Ronnie was
very proud of them. He thought
he'd try them out on a peanut
someone had dropped on the
kitchen floor, and brought his foot
down **CRASH!** on to the tiles.

The noise was music to Ronnie's ears and he decided that stamping was the greatest thing in the world.

Next day Ronnie stamped on an empty orange-juice carton which gave a very pleasing **POP!** and made several girls scream.

Then he spied an empty Coke can. It made a terrific **BANG!** when Ronnie stamped on it, and nearly made a boy fall off his bike.

A half-full packet of crisps outside Ronnie's gate wasn't quite so satisfactory, but the smashed crisps crackled enough to frighten Ronnie's cat, Charlie.

There was nothing on the kitchen floor for Ronnie to stamp on so he blew up a paper bag, tied the top with a rubber band and jumped on it. It made the best **BoP!** ever.

Mrs Stiltskin was so frightened she dropped a pan of chips, and Mr Stiltskin accidentally tore his newspaper in half.

Charlie the cat thought seriously about moving in with the people next door, a nice old couple who never made a noise.

"Ronnie!" roared Mr Stiltskin. "This stamping has got to stop!"

Yes, Dad.

But after tea he saw that his mother had dropped a grape right in front of the kitchen sink, so he stamped on that. *Smush! Squish!* Seeds and green flesh shot across the floor and stuck to the wall.

"Ronnie!" screamed Mrs Stiltskin. "Stop stamping! You know what happened to Rumpel!"

After this Ronnie tried not to
stamp for a whole day.

But then he went to his friend
Bob's birthday party, and there
were all these balloons lying about,
just asking to be stamped on.

Bob's granny thought another war had started and her legs gave way completely.
But Ronnie was having such a good time bursting balloons, he didn't hear Bob's mother shouting at him. He didn't even see Bob's granny being carried upstairs.

When Mrs Stiltskin came to collect Ronnie, Bob's mother said, "We don't want Ronnie round here any more."

CHARLIE LEAVES HOME

Mrs Stiltskin thought that Ronnie
had learned his lesson. But he hadn't.
On the way home from Bob's
house, he stamped on an ice-cream
someone had dropped. It stuck to
his boots and he walked it all over
the hall carpet.

Mrs Stiltskin took Ronnie's boots away and made him wear his slippers. But he stamped on a nail that went right through to his foot.

The doctor said Ronnie ought to wear boots if he was the sort of boy who stamped on things.

Mrs Stiltskin tried to explain how noisy boots were, but the doctor said, "It's better than having holes in your feet."

Mr and Mrs Stiltskin became very depressed. They made Ronnie stay in the garden as much as possible. At least the noise wasn't so close.

Ronnie stamped on stones…  CRUNCH!

 FLUMPH! he stamped on molehills…

and bonfires, on dustbin lids…  CLANG!

 CRACK! and broken flower pots, and clothes pegs.

He even stamped on the crazy paving, and made it really crazy.

Charlie the cat spent the
day at the top of a very
tall tree.

When Mr and Mrs Stiltskin let
Ronnie in for the night, they
made him take
off his boots and
leave them
outside.

But before he
went to bed,
Ronnie stamped
on his pillow
to make it comfy;

he stamped on the
toothpaste tube
to make the tooth-
paste ooze out;

and he stamped
on his clothes
so that they should
be nicely pressed
for the morning.

Mr and Mrs Stiltskin went quite hoarse from shouting at Ronnie. Their throats were so sore, they couldn't speak for a whole day, and had to write notes to each other.

Charlie the cat went to live with the people next door.

A DANGEROUS PLACE

The people who lived in Ronnie's
street became very unfriendly,
so the Stiltskins decided to move
away. They bought an old cottage,
outside town, where there were
no neighbours to complain about
the noise.

Mr Stiltskin had to build a new kitchen. The old one was too small and the floorboards were rotten. He bricked up the doors and warned Ronnie to keep away.

But Ronnie couldn't resist taking
a peek. The windows had fallen
out and wet leaves had floated in,
making the room wet and musty.
Hundreds of tiny creatures had
made their homes in damp, dark
corners.

Ronnie climbed through the broken window and tried out the floorboards.

What a delicious noise! Ronnie sang with joy.

Soon a trail of wounded and unhappy creatures began to leave the old kitchen. Their homes were gone (not to mention their children). Ronnie didn't even notice them. He was having such fun.

And then a voice said:

Ronnie, caught in mid-stamp, saw a little man looking through the broken window. He wore a red nightcap and his long nose rested on the sill. His skin was as wrinkled as a prune.

"All this stamping has got to stop," said the little man. "I know it's fun, but it never does you any good. I learned the hard way."

Who's going to stop me?

The millipede.

"Millipedes aren't dangerous," scoffed Ronnie. "They're teeny weeny things."

"They grow," the stranger told him. "They grow to be ENORMOUS. And they've got hundreds and hundreds of feet. I wouldn't like you to come to grief!"

And with that he vanished.

Ronnie peered into the shadowy corners of the old kitchen. He began to imagine giant THINGS lurking there, and ran out, fast.

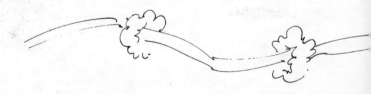

"I just saw a tiny man with a wrinkled face," panted Ronnie, "and he was wearing a red hat like a sock. He told me there was a giant millipede living here."

"Sounds like Rumpel Stiltskin," said Ronnie's father. "But he died four hundred years ago. And as for giant millipedes, they live only in jungles."

Ronnie wasn't so sure. He decided that if millipedes grew to be enormous, he'd better stop them growing before they got too big to handle.

RONNIE MAKES A PROMISE

Later that day, Ronnie saw a
millipede slipping between the milk
bottles on the step. He swung his
foot out – but too late to get the
millipede. Too late to avoid the
bottles. Crack! Tinkle! They flew
into the air and smashed on to the
path.

While he was sweeping up the
broken glass, Ronnie saw the
millipede creeping under a ladder.
Ronnie dropped his broom and
leapt for the millipede.

He missed the millipede but he didn't miss the ladder. *CLONK!* *SMASH!* It slipped down the wall and went straight through the sitting-room window.

"We were going to take you to the seaside this weekend," said Mr Stiltskin. "But not if you do any more stamping."

We've had enough!

The beach was one of Ronnie's favourite places. There were so many things to stamp on. Limpets to CRUNCH! shells to CRACK! old cans to BANG! and pools to SPLOSH! in. How could Ronnie bear to miss it?

"I promise not to stamp on anything again," said Ronnie breathlessly.

He closed his eyes, wondering how he could keep his promise.

RONNIE MEETS RUMPEL

Ronnie didn't stamp on anything
for the rest of that day. But it was
agony. His feet ached with not
stamping. They itched and burned
and throbbed with not treading
hard on anything.

At teatime Ronnie had to twist his feet round the legs of his chair so they wouldn't be tempted by so much as a crumb.

Have you got toothacke, Ronnie?

No, but my feet are killing me.

When he went to bed he dreamed that he had the biggest feet in the world, and they THUMPED! and BOOMED! even when he walked on tiptoe.

"Wake up!" said a cross voice.

Ronnie opened his eyes. There, sitting on the end of his bed, was the little man in the red nightcap. "Are ... are you Rumpel Stiltskin?" Ronnie asked.

"Right first time," said the little man. "I came to warn you, Ronnie. Don't you remember my story?"

"There was a girl, and she asked me to spin flax into gold for her, so that the King would marry her. I agreed and she promised to give me her first child as a reward."

"That wretched girl broke her word. The King married her but she refused to hand over their baby. So I gave her another chance; I said if she guessed my name in three days she could keep the child."

"Well, she guessed right. I was that mad I stamped so hard I went right through the floor. Down, down, down I fell into a deep, dark pit!"

"It's taken me hundreds of years to recover," said Rumpel. "So let that be a warning." He wagged a bony finger and scuttled to the door.

"Hold on," said Ronnie.

"What was all that about a giant millipede?"

Rumpel gave Ronnie a funny wink, and then he vanished.

Ronnie lay in bed thinking about what his ancestor had told him. He tried to keep his feet still, but they had a mind of their own.

CLANK! CLONK! CLANK! CLONK! went the bedsprings.

His father banged on the wall.

Ronnie, be quiet or you won't go to the beach!

Please!

And then Ronnie had a brilliant idea. He would go to the old kitchen. It was right on the other side of the house and he could make as much noise as he wanted. His parents would never hear him. As for giant millipedes – they lived only in jungles – didn't they? Why should he believe a tiny man who was hundreds of years old?

A MIDNIGHT RUMPUS

Ronnie tiptoed past his parents'
bedroom, carrying his boots. He
didn't even have to switch the light
on, because it was such a bright
moonlit night.

In the kitchen he lifted the bag out of the waste-bin; it was full of lovely things to stamp on. Ronnie put it over his shoulder and crept out of the house.

When he reached the window of the *old* kitchen, he poured his rubbish across the floor. Cartons, cans, boxes, bottles, polythene packaging and empty kitchen towel tubes were spread before him like a feast.

47

Ronnie pulled on his boots.
"Yippee!" he yelled and leapt
through the window.

Ronnie bounced, stamped, crashed,
cracked and shrieked with glee.

A deafening rumpus poured from
the old kitchen, but no one heard it.

Creatures buzzed, screamed,
whizzed and fluttered in all
directions, but no one heard them.
And no one heard Ronnie's howl
of delight or the dreadful thudding
of his murderous black boots.

All too soon everything had been
smashed so flat that no sound could
be heard except for a pathetic
SQUISH! SQUASH! SQUIDDLE! And a long
sigh from the tired old floorboards.

And then Ronnie saw the
millipede. It was right in the middle
of the floor, bathed in moonlight.

Ronnie couldn't help himself.
With a mighty spring he leapt
towards the tiny creature. But the
millipede rolled to safety and
Ronnie crashed onto empty
floorboards.

The old boards split. And down
went Ronnie, into a deep, dark pit!

THE MILLIPEDE'S REVENGE

As Ronnie lay there, staring up at the hole he'd tumbled through, something moved into the path of moonlight. Something HUGE!

Clinging to a thick cobweb the *thing* began to swing down towards Ronnie. Closer and closer. And now Ronnie could see that it had hundreds of feet. Hundreds and hundreds and hundreds.

It was a giant millipede!

"Oooooo! P-p-please don't stamp on me. I didn't mean to hurt your baby. Honestly I didn't!"

But the millipede kept coming.

No one heard him. And with one last dreadful wail, the terrified Ronnie fainted clean away.

Next morning Mr and Mrs Stiltskin
searched for Ronnie everywhere.
They called and called, but Ronnie
couldn't answer – he'd lost his voice.
In the end they rang the police. And
then Mr Stiltskin remembered the
old kitchen.

When they pulled Ronnie out of
the cellar he was covered in bruises
– six hundred and fifty, to be precise.

A millipede
stamped on me.

Mr Stiltskin was not sympathetic.
"You fell into a cellar full of junk,
that's what you did," he said. "I told
you that place was dangerous,
didn't I?"

"Yes, Dad," whispered Ronnie.

The newspapers heard of Ronnie's ordeal and printed his story.

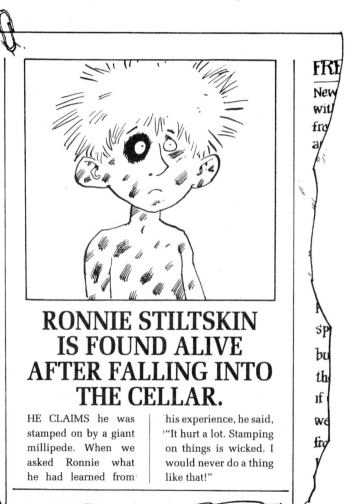

RONNIE STILTSKIN IS FOUND ALIVE AFTER FALLING INTO THE CELLAR.

HE CLAIMS he was stamped on by a giant millipede. When we asked Ronnie what he had learned from his experience, he said, '"It hurt a lot. Stamping on things is wicked. I would never do a thing like that!"

Ronnie never stamped on anything again. And he never saw Rumpel Stiltskin.

Except once!

More SPRINTERS for you to enjoy!

- *Little Stupendo Flies High* Jon Blake   0-7445-5970-7

- *Captain Abdul's Pirate School* Colin McNaughton 0-7445-5242-7

- *The Ghost in Annie's Room* Philippa Pearce   0-7445-5993-6

- *Molly and the Beanstalk* Pippa Goodhart   0-7445-5981-2

- *Taking the Cat's Way Home* Jan Mark   0-7445-8268-7

- *The Finger-eater* Dick King-Smith   0-7445-8269-5

- *Care of Henry* Anne Fine   0-7445-8270-9

- *The Impossible Parents Go Green* Brian Patten   0-7445-7881-7

- *Flora's Fantastic Revenge* Nick Warburton   0-7445-7898-1

- *Jolly Roger* Colin McNaughton   0-7445-8293-8

- *The Haunting of Pip Parker* Anne Fine   0-7445-8294-6

- *Tarquin the Wonder Horse* June Crebbin   0-7445-7882-5

- *Cup Final Kid* Martin Waddell   0-7445-8297-0

- *Lady Long-legs* Jan Mark   0-7445-8296-2

- *Ronnie and the Giant Millipede* Jenny Nimmo   0-7445-8298-9

All at £3.99

TARQUIN THE WONDER HORSE

There are times when Tarquin's special magic only brings trouble! Will he manage to live happily ever after?

June Crebbin was a primary school teacher before taking early retirement to concentrate on her writing. She is the author of a number of books for children, including *Emmelina and the Monster*, *The Curse of the Skull* and several volumes of verse. A frequent visitor to primary schools, where she gives readings, talks and workshops, June Crebbin lives in Leicestershire with her husband and her rabbit.

JUNE CREBBIN

TARQUIN THE WONDER HORSE

Illustrations by Tony Ross

TED SMART

For Gail and David
and
Somerby Equestrian Centre

First published 2000 by
Walker Books Ltd, 87 Vauxhall Walk
London SE11 5HJ

This edition produced 2002 for
The Book People Ltd, Hall Wood Avenue,
Haydock, St Helens WA11 9UL

2 4 6 8 10 9 7 5 3 1

Text © 2000 June Crebbin
Illustrations © 2000 Tony Ross

This book has been typeset in Garamond

Printed and bound in Great Britain by
The Guernsey Press Co. Ltd

British Library Cataloguing in Publication Data:
a catalogue record for this book
is available from the British Library

ISBN 0-7445-7882-5

Contents

Chapter One

Once, a horse, weary of travelling in far-off countries, decided to return home. As his ship pulled into the harbour, he thought, the first thing I must do is find a job. But I'll say nothing of my magic powers. They only bring trouble.

Still, he decided to use his power
of speech.

In the market he approached a
farmer. "Are you looking for a good,
strong worker?" he asked.

The farmer, though extremely
surprised to hear the horse speak,
knew a bargain when he saw one
and hired him on the spot.

Tarquin, that was the horse's
name, settled quickly into his new
home. His workday was long and
hard. But in the quiet evenings, he
enjoyed the company
of a grey mouse. She
told him about the fat
farm cat and its
attempts to catch her.

12

"Mind you," said the mouse,
"I don't go in the house. I'm not
stupid. Though sometimes, I can't
help wishing for a piece of cheese."

And that's when Tarquin should
have kept quiet.

Outside, the farmer, who was
passing by, heard him say: "I can
grant your wish. Take hold of a
single strand of my mane, pull it
out and speak your heart's desire.
Be careful not to *break* the strand,
or the magic will be undone."

Well, the mouse nipped up Tarquin's leg, took hold of a single strand of mane – and pulled.

At once, the hair changed into a chunk of cheese.

"There's plenty more where that came from!" laughed Tarquin.

The farmer trembled with excitement.

More where that came from? he thought. I should say! I could wish for gold. A gold piece for every strand! But I must think carefully. That horse is strong and he might not want to give up *all* his mane.

He hurried into the farmhouse.

Some time later, a smile spread across his face.

Chapter Two

Early next morning, the farmer
mixed some special herbs into
Tarquin's food.

When Tarquin ate breakfast he
began to feel sleepy and soon he
slumped to the floor.

The farmer brought a sack, put on thick gloves, and pulled and pulled until Tarquin's whole mane was his.

Laughing, he carried it into the farmhouse.

He took hold of a single strand of hair. "I wish for a piece of gold!" he cried.

At once the hair changed into a gold piece.

The farmer grabbed a handful of
hair. "I wish for ten pieces of gold
for every strand!" he shouted.

At once, gold pieces filled his
hands.

The farmer shook with excitement.
He grabbed up the rest of the mane
in his arms.

"I wish for a thousand – no, a MILLION – pieces of gold for every strand!" he yelled.

At once, gold pieces appeared all
over the kitchen. Like drops of
golden rain, they poured down onto
the floor. The farmer scooped them
up in his hands. He let them trickle
like water through his fingers.

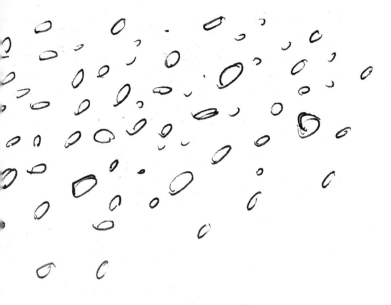

"I'm rich! I'm rich!" he cried.

The gold kept coming.

The farmer was up to his knees –

"All mine!" he shouted.

The gold rose higher. Now the farmer was up to his waist ... his chest –

"That's enough!" he protested, laughing. "Stop! Stop!"

The farmer could hardly breathe. The gold was crushing him.

He tried to think. There'd been a warning. Something the horse had said... "Be careful not to *break* the strand..."

The farmer noticed one last strand of hair that he had missed before. He managed to reach it, and quickly pulled it in two.

At once, the kitchen fell silent. Even the birds outside stopped singing. When they started again a moment later, all the gold had gone.

*　*　*

All day, Tarquin lay in a deep sleep.
At last, towards evening, he stirred.

The mouse crept from her corner.

Tarquin lifted his head. His neck
felt strangely light.

"The farmer took your mane," the
mouse told him. "He must know of
your magic."

"Then I cannot stay," said Tarquin.

Sadly, he said goodbye to his
friend, left the farm and set out on
his travels once more.

Chapter Three

Snow began to fall as Tarquin left the village. Soon it was difficult to see where he was going.

That night, he huddled by a hedge.

The next morning, the snow had
stopped but the road was icy and
since there was no one about,
Tarquin drew in his breath – and
blew.

Out of his nostrils shot twin blasts
of fire. At once, the ice in front of
him melted. Tarquin stepped
forward eagerly. Surely he would
find a friendly farmhouse soon?

High on the crest of a hill, a woman was watching Tarquin's fiery progress. She was Gelda, the Queen's cousin, out hunting the rare snow eagle.

"A fire-breathing horse!" she murmured excitedly.

She gave her huntsmen orders to abandon the search for the snow eagle, and capture the horse instead. "Be careful!" she snapped. "I don't want him frightened." Then she sped back to her palace.

"Prepare the Master Stable!" she ordered. "Put out the golden hay net, but bring the silver drinking bucket to me."

Chapter Four

So Tarquin awoke the next morning
not in a farmhouse, but in a royal
palace. He was taken to Gelda,
where a silver bucket was placed
before him. He was desperate for
a drink.

But the bucket was full of ice.
"How am I to drink this?" he asked.
"Oh, you can speak!" cried Gelda.
"I need water, not
ice," said Tarquin.

"Then *melt* it!"
shrieked Gelda.
"Like you
melted it
yesterday!"
Tarquin's heart
sank.

"Think of the posters!" cried Gelda. "IS IT A HORSE OR IS IT A DRAGON? COME AND SEE THE ONLY FIRE-BREATHING HORSE IN THE WORLD! Two shows nightly."

"No, thank you," said Tarquin.

He turned to leave.

"Stop him!" yelled Gelda.

Tarquin felt the points of a dozen deadly swords.

"It wouldn't be safe," he warned. "Things could go wrong."

Chapter Five

At seven o'clock that night, the crowds assembled in the Palace Theatre. The band, sitting just in front of the stage, played a few rousing marches. Then the announcer cried: "Ladies and Gentlemen, allow me to introduce Tarquin – the Dragon Horse!"

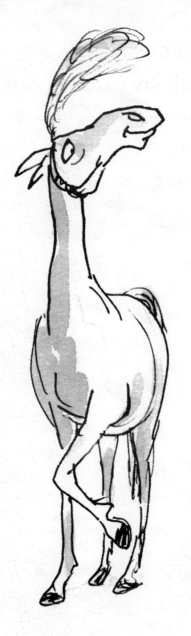

On came
Tarquin, with
a plume on his
head and his
hooves painted
gold.

The announcer
stood up.

"First," he cried,
"Tarquin will
light the birthday
candles!"

On to the stage came a small girl carrying a cake with six candles. She placed it on a table and stood back.

Tarquin drew in his breath.

He blew – very, very gently.

All six candles lit.

The crowd cheered.

Next, five unlit torches were
brought on, each in its own stand.
Tarquin drew in his breath. He
blew – not quite so gently this time.
All five torches lit.
The crowd roared.

"And finally!" cried the announcer.
"The Leap of Fire! Not only will
Tarquin light the hoop, he will then
leap through it!"

The crowd quietened.

An enormous hoop, covered in
paper, was brought on. The
drummers began their drum roll.

Tarquin drew in his breath. He
blew – hard and long.

Twin blasts of fire shot straight
through the hoop of paper to the very
edge of the stage. Flames licked the
sheets of music that the band was
playing. They caught alight.

"FIRE!" shouted the trumpeter.

"FIRE!" yelled the tuba player.

The Royal Fire Officers rushed in
with buckets and hoses.

Water gushed everywhere. Hats
were soaked, dresses drenched,
trousers sodden.

Every time Gelda opened her

mouth to scream an order, she got
a jet of water in it.

Showers bounced off drums.
Flutes spurted fountains. The tuba
filled up like a giant teacup.

Tarquin quietly made his way
down the back stairs, out of the
palace and into the night.

Chapter Six

That's it, thought Tarquin. No more getting mixed up with *people*.

He spent that night in the middle of a forest. It was very cold. But in the morning he woke to bright sunshine and the snow was melting fast.

He stretched. It was lovely to feel the warmth on his back.

"Oh, what a beautiful morning!" he sang, going to drink at a nearby stream. "Oh, what a beautiful day!"

The water tasted good.

Behind him, a twig broke. He swung round.

A girl stared. Then from behind the trees, a boy appeared.

The girl said, "I'm Rosanna. He's Paul. Are you a magic horse?"

At once, Tarquin was on his guard.

"It's just that you have golden hooves," said Rosanna.

"And a splendid plume," said Paul.

Tarquin snorted.

"And you sing beautifully!" said Rosanna. "So we thought you must be magic."

Tarquin pawed the ground. He remembered what he'd decided yesterday: *No more getting mixed up with people.* But these children didn't seem so bad.

"I'm Tarquin," he said.

"Please, we need your help," said
Paul. He kept looking behind him.

For the first time, Tarquin noticed
they were frightened.

Suddenly, there was a great roar.

SEVENTY-ONE
SEVENTY-TWO
I'M GETTING
HUNGRY

The children clung
to each other.

"It's the Ogre!"
they sobbed.

"There isn't much
time," said Rosanna
urgently. "We're
supposed to be
hiding. The Ogre

wanted to play hide-and-seek before
breakfast."

"That sounds fun!" said Tarquin.
"That's a good game!"

"It isn't!" cried Paul.

And then Tarquin realized – it
wasn't a game. The children were
the Ogre's breakfast.

NINETY-EIGHT NINETY-NINE A HUNDRED

"You could save us," begged Rosanna. "You could carry us away."

READY OR NOT!

roared the Ogre.

"He's coming! He's coming!" screamed Paul.

Chapter Seven

"Jump on my back!" cried Tarquin.
Rosanna and Paul leapt up.

Just as the Ogre crashed into the
clearing, Tarquin was away.

Behind them came a howl of rage:
"You won't get far!"

The Ogre set off after them, covering
the ground in mighty strides.

"Faster! Faster!" urged Rosanna.
But Tarquin couldn't. The forest
was too thick. He had to look for
paths between the trees.

The Ogre was gaining on them.

If anything got in his way, he
simply struck it to one side.

Rosanna glanced behind. He was
almost on them. "Oh Tarquin, I
wish you could fly!" she cried.

At that moment, Tarquin swerved to avoid a rabbit hole. Rosanna clutched at his newly growing mane – and a single strand of hair came loose... Tarquin's shoulder muscles slowly rippled outwards, on and on, until they weren't muscles at all, but huge silver wings.

Up, up soared the horse and the
children, leaving the Ogre crashing
with anger below.

Over the forest they flew, and away.

Rosanna leaned forward. "There!" she cried. "Can you see? By the lake, at the foot of the mountain. That's our village."

As they flew closer, people came running out to greet them.

Tarquin landed softly. The children tumbled off.

"Tarquin," whispered Rosanna, leading him forward to meet her family and friends, "you're a Wonder!"

Tarquin still lives in the village. He helps with the ploughing and the haymaking. He's a strong and willing worker, and he keeps the Ogre away. No one ever dreams of plucking out a strand of his mane.

Except the children, of course. Just now and then.

More SPRINTERS for you to enjoy!

- *Little Stupendo Flies High* Jon Blake   0-7445-5970-7

- *Captain Abdul's Pirate School* Colin McNaughton 0-7445-5242-7

- *The Ghost in Annie's Room* Philippa Pearce   0-7445-5993-6

- *Molly and the Beanstalk* Pippa Goodhart   0-7445-5981-2

- *Taking the Cat's Way Home* Jan Mark   0-7445-8268-7

- *The Finger-eater* Dick King-Smith   0-7445-8269-5

- *Care of Henry* Anne Fine   0-7445-8270-9

- *The Impossible Parents Go Green* Brian Patten   0-7445-7881-7

- *Flora's Fantastic Revenge* Nick Warburton   0-7445-7898-1

- *Jolly Roger* Colin McNaughton   0-7445-8293-8

- *The Haunting of Pip Parker* Anne Fine   0-7445-8294-6

- *Tarquin the Wonder Horse* June Crebbin   0-7445-7882-5

All at £3.99

MOLLY AND THE BEANSTALK

Little Molly could never have imagined what awaits her at the top of the beanstalk!

Molly and the Beanstalk is Pippa Goodhart's first title for Walker. She has written many other books for young and older readers, including *Flow*, shortlisted for the Smarties Prize, and *Ginny's Egg*, shortlisted for the Young Telegraph Book of the Year. However, Pippa has not always known she wanted to be a writer. She says of her school years, "I was slow to learn to read (I can still remember the agony) and so poor at spelling that I thought I was bad at writing." She did not let her early experiences put her off however, and worked for several years in bookshops before becoming a full-time writer. She now lives in Leicester with her husband Mick, an architect, and their three children.

PIPPA GOODHART

Molly and the Beanstalk

Illustrations by Brita Granström

TED SMART

*For all the children at
Overdale Infant School in Leicester
P.G.*

First published 2001 by Walker Books Ltd
87 Vauxhall Walk, London SE11 5HJ

This edition produced 2002 for
The Book People Ltd, Hall Wood Avenue,
Haydock, St Helens WA11 9UL

2 4 6 8 10 9 7 5 3 1

Text © 2001 Pippa Goodhart
Illustrations © 2001 Brita Granström

This book has been typeset in Garamond

Printed and bound in Great Britain
by The Guernsey Press Co. Ltd

British Library Cataloguing in Publication Data:
a catalogue record for this book
is available from the British Library

ISBN 0-7445-5981-2

Contents

Chapter One

Molly and Old Ma Coddle lived on
a little farm with Sylvie Cow, some
hens and a few ducks on a pond.

Molly would look over the fence
to the world beyond and wonder,
What would it be like to see new
places and meet new people?

Molly knew that there was more in the world than the world she knew because Old Ma told her stories. She told stories about giants and magic and much more.

It was spring. Old Ma and Molly seeded and weeded and sowed and hoed.

"I wish I could sow a story seed," said Molly.

"Well, wishes are a kind of seed," said Old Ma.

"So, am I sowing a seed just by wishing?"

"Maybe you are," said Old Ma. "Look at the sky, Molly. I think a story *might* just be starting. The clouds are melting away. Something strange is happening to the weather."

Chapter Two

Day after day, the sun shone in the sky, hotter and hotter. The seeds began to sprout, but their green stems soon shrivelled as the earth baked dry.

Sylvie Cow's tail swung to swat away the flies as she stood in the shade and chewed on the few blades of grass she could find. Molly leaned against her soft side. "Oh, it's hot, hot, hot," she said.

Molly and Old Ma struggled from the pond to the fields with buckets of water. But even the pond was drying out and the ducks had flown away.

"This is horrible," said Molly. "If this is part of my story, I don't like it."

Old Ma mopped her face with a flap of apron. "But Molly," she said, "most stories have to start with a bad bit. If they didn't, then how could things get better and end happily?"

Molly's story got worse. The sun shone hotter and Sylvie Cow got thinner and thinner. There was no milk, no butter, no cheese. Old Ma got thinner too. She got ill.

There were no vegetables and no fruit and the hungry hens had stopped laying eggs.

"We'll starve!" said Molly.

"You must go and sell some of our things," said Old Ma. "We need money to buy food if we can't grow it ourselves."

So Molly put on her sunhat and walked to market with a wheelbarrow full of plates and jugs and pictures.

She sold them all for a fistful of coins. Then she used the money to buy bread and cheese and honey and a small bundle of hay. She walked wearily home.

"At least we won't be hungry now," Molly told Sylvie Cow as she fed her the hay. "And perhaps my story will start to get better."

Chapter Three

But in a few days they had eaten all
the bread and cheese and honey
and hay. More days passed and still
the sun shone hot and no rain fell.
Sylvie Cow's ribs showed. Molly was
thin too.

Old Ma just stayed in bed, and that frightened Molly.

"What do I do now, Old Ma?" asked Molly. "I don't want this story any more. Can't we just stop it and go back to normal?"

But Old Ma shook
her poor tired head.
"You can't stop a
story once it's
started," she said.

"A story isn't a story
unless it has a beginning and a
middle and an end."

Molly sighed. "But what can I do
to hurry it on to a better bit?"

"You must sell Sylvie
Cow," said Old Ma.

"Oh no!" said Molly.
"I love Sylvie Cow."

"I do too, Molly,
but Sylvie Cow is
all we have left."

So Molly slipped a rope around Sylvie's curly horns, and she led her to the market in town.

Chapter Four

The butcher in town looked at
Sylvie Cow and offered Molly shiny
coins. But Molly saw the butcher's
shiny sharp knife, and she turned
and ran with Sylvie Cow, away and
away and up into green hills.

Molly told Sylvie Cow, "I wish we could stay here in the hills.

There's all the grass that you could ever eat and I'm sure there's food for people too." But Molly remembered poor Old Ma, ill and hungry at home. "I can't stay," she said. "And if I leave you here, who will look after you?"

Molly looked up and saw a boy
in a tree.

"Who are you?" she asked.

"I'm Jack," said the boy. "I'd give
your cow the best grass and I'd
milk her every morning and
evening."

"Would you talk to her too?" asked Molly.

"I would," said Jack. "I have nobody else to talk to."

"I have," said Molly. "I've got Old Ma at home. But the weather has gone wrong and nothing will grow and we have nothing to eat.

If you bought Sylvie Cow, then I could buy food for Old Ma and me."

But Jack shook his head. "I can't buy your cow. I have no money. Look!" He jumped down from the tree and pulled his pockets inside out. All that came out was one bean.

Molly looked at the lush green grass all around. She looked at poor Sylvie's tired drooping head. She looked at Jack's kind eyes – and she decided.

"You can have Sylvie Cow if you give me the bean. Just so long as you love her and give her back to me when the weather comes right."

So Molly hugged
Sylvie Cow's bony
neck and promised
to have her home
soon. Then she left
her with Jack.

Molly ran all the
way back to her hot bare home
where the sun still shone and Old
Ma was still ill in bed.

Chapter Five

Molly told Old Ma about the lush green grass in the hills. "I left Sylvie Cow with Jack. They will be happy."

"And what did this Jack boy pay for the cow?" asked Old Ma.

Molly showed her the bean.

"One mean little bean!" shouted Old Ma, sitting up in bed. "You gave away our Sylvie Cow for one hard little bean? Oh Molly!" And Old Ma wobbled up from her bed and went to the window and threw the bean out.

Molly began to cry, and she ran outside, away from cross Old Ma. She found the bean on the ground. She knelt down beside it and she cried with hunger and hurt. She sobbed, "Oh, I don't want to be in this story any more! Please make it stop!"

What Molly didn't see was that her tears watered the earth, and the bean began to grow.

What Molly didn't know was that her story had got to its middle. Things were about to change.

Chapter Six

Molly lay in bed, too unhappy
and hungry to sleep. She thought
about the bean. Perhaps she could
clean it and nibble it and fill a
little of her hungry tummy?

So she lit a lantern and went
searching the dark for the purple
dot of bean.

She looked on the ground, but
what she found made her tip back
her head and look up, up and up.

"WOW!"
said Molly.
"A beanstalk
that's bigger
than a tree!"
And Molly
thought of the
enormous
beans that
must grow
somewhere at
the top of
that stalk.

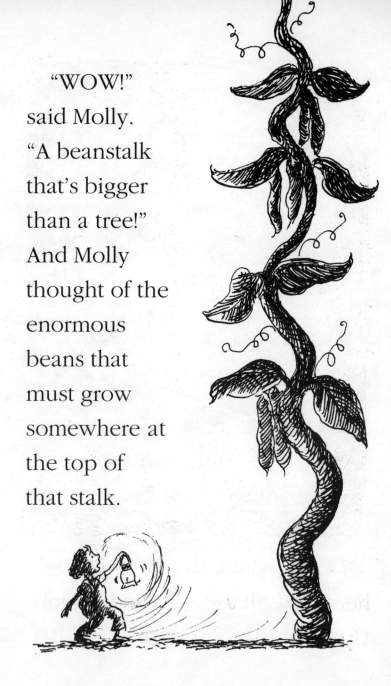

Molly put the lantern between
her teeth, and she began to climb.
Up and up and up until ...

a dazzle of bright light made her
drop the lantern in surprise and
cover her eyes.

Molly saw giant orange flowers
and giant green beans. Then she
saw something else; something that
moved. She looked up and up
again and saw...

Chapter Seven

"A GIANT!" said Molly.

"No," said the giant. "I'm just a girl. My name is Molly. But *what* and *who* are you?"

"I'm Molly too," said Molly. "I live down there on the farm," and she pointed.

The giant Molly bent down close and poked little Molly with one finger. "Are you real?" she asked.

"Of course I am!" said Molly. "I must be, because I'm hungry! And so is Old Ma. It's been hot, hot, hot and our plants have died and Sylvie Cow has gone.

We're starving. But one of your big beans could feed us for a week. Please, could I take one?"

"I don't think you can," said the giant Molly. "They're just the pattern on my bed cover."

She picked up giant pens and
paper and scissors, and she drew
and she cut and she gave Molly
some beans so big she had to
hug them.

"Thank you!" said Molly. "You are kind."

"Well, I want to help you," said the giant Molly.

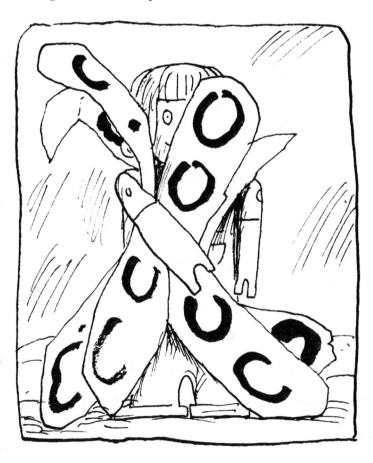

"I think that your weather going wrong might have been my fault," she continued. "I've been hot, hot, hot with a fever. But I think I'm better now. Maybe that means things will get better for you too?"

 "Oh yes!" Molly pointed. "Look down there! There are clouds again. It's raining! Everything will grow again now. I think my story must be getting near the end. Please, could you put everything back as it should be?"

Chapter Eight

Next morning the giant Molly
picked up Sylvie Cow and Jack and
she put them back at the farm.

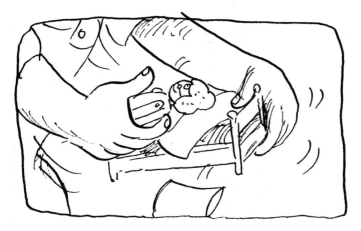

She took Old Ma from her bed
and put her in the doorway.

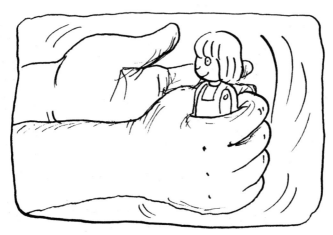

And, very gently, she put Molly
back on the ground.

Chapter Nine

The rain made everything fresh and
green again. Old Ma and Molly
made bean soup and bean salad,
bean fritters and bean cake, and
they decorated the farm with giant
orange bean flowers.

Jack milked Sylvie Cow

and he
skimmed cream

and
slapped butter

and pressed cheese.

When their feast was ready, they
sang and they danced and they ate
and they drank.

Then they were tired and it was
time to sit and tell stories.

Jack told the first one. It was a
sad story of how he came to have
no home and no family.

Then Molly said, "Why don't you stay and live with us? You could be my brother and Old Ma could be your granny."

"I'd like that, Jack," said Old Ma. "So would I," said Jack, and he smiled.

Then Molly told a story called *Molly and the Beanstalk.*

"Does it end with 'they all lived happily ever after'?" asked Old Ma.

And they did.

More *Sprinters* for you to enjoy!

- *Little Stupendo Flies High* Jon Blake   0-7445-5970-7
- *Captain Abdul's Pirate School* Colin McNaughton 0-7445-5242-7
- *The Ghost in Annie's Room* Philippa Pearce   0-7445-5993-6
- *Molly and the Beanstalk* Pippa Goodhart   0-7445-5981-2
- *Taking the Cat's Way Home* Jan Mark   0-7445-8268-7
- *The Finger-eater* Dick King-Smith   0-7445-8269-5
- *Care of Henry* Anne Fine   0-7445-8270-9
- *The Impossible Parents Go Green* Brian Patten   0-7445-7881-7
- *Flora's Fantastic Revenge* Nick Warburton   0-7445-7898-1
- *Jolly Roger* Colin McNaughton   0-7445-8293-8
- *The Haunting of Pip Parker* Anne Fine   0-7445-8294-6
- *Tarquin the Wonder Horse* June Crebbin   0-7445-7882-5

All at £3.99

FLORA'S FANTASTIC REVENGE

Nick Warburton was a primary school teacher for ten years before deciding to become a full-time writer. He has written plays for stage, television and radio, including *Conversations from the Engine Room*, which won the 1985 Radio Times Drama Award. He has also written a number of children's books, among them *The Battle of Baked Bean Alley*, *Normal Nesbitt*, *Dennis Dipp on Gilbert's Pond* and *Lost In Africa*. A Visiting Fellow of Chichester University, Nick is married with a son and lives in Cambridge.

NICK WARBURTON

Illustrations by Cathy Gale

TED SMART

For Freddie

First published 2000 by
Walker Books Ltd, 87 Vauxhall Walk
London SE11 5HJ

This edition produced 2002 for
The Book People Ltd, Hall Wood Avenue,
Haydock, St Helens WA11 9UL

2 4 6 8 10 9 7 5 3 1

Text © 2000 Nick Warburton
Illustrations © 2000, 2001 Cathy Gale

The right of Nick Warburton to be identified as author of this
work has been asserted by him in accordance with the
Copyright, Designs and Patents Act 1988

This book has been typeset in Garamond

Printed and bound in Great Britain by The Guernsey Press Co. Ltd

British Library Cataloguing in Publication Data:
a catalogue record for this book is
available from the British Library

ISBN 0-7445-7898-1

CONTENTS

LURKING AND LISTENING

Emma and Will were watching Mr
Petchy pottering about in his front
garden. Mr Petchy had a very big
front garden because he lived in
the big house on the corner.

He was getting ready for his Flower Show. He had a flower show every year and invited everyone to come and see the most amazing plants.

"The plants are so amazing because he has green fingers," Emma said.

"Green fingers?" said Will. "You mean they're not ripe?"

"No. It means he has a special way with plants, that's all."

But as Mr Petchy pottered about, Will thought there really *was* a faint green tinge to his fingers.

They watched him working away
at his plants and putting up stalls for
games and cakes and toffee-apples.
It isn't just plants he has a special
way with, thought Will.

They watched him fill his
watering-can from an overgrown,
dark-green pond.

Mr Petchy's Flower Show raised money for charity, so of course, Will and Emma liked to do their bit.

Last year they'd grown some seeds, but Trevor Tapp had poured something nasty in the flowerpot when they weren't looking.

Big, brawny Trevor Tapp lived over the road. He liked spoiling things. Will and Emma's plants came up weedy and floppy, and nobody bought them.

The year before that, they'd made
some buns, but Trevor Tapp had
slipped something nasty in the
mixture and the buns turned out all
wrong. The vicar bought one and
then went behind the first-aid tent
to be sick. So they didn't make
much money then, either.

They thought they'd try something different this year.

"I know," said Will. "We can clean windows for people."

But Trevor Tapp was lurking and listening. He heard every word, and sniggered and rubbed his hands.

WINDOWS BIG AND SMALL

Windows cleaned by Will and Emma. Very cheap. For charity.

Will and Emma went home to make a sign for their new business. They propped it by the front gate and went indoors to wait for their first customer.

They waited ... and waited.
Nobody came.

So they went back outside to see
where everyone was. Across the
road they saw a big, brawny boy
cleaning windows. It was Trevor
Tapp, busily spoiling their plans.

"Oh well," Emma said. "Maybe we can share the windows with Trevor. Pop over and speak to him about it."

"He'll turn nasty and slosh water over me," said Will. "He's that kind of boy."

"He might not."

Will sighed and crossed the road.
Trevor Tapp saw him coming and
sloshed water over him.

"Don't mind me," he laughed.
"I'm only having a bit of fun!"
Will trudged back, dripping wet.
"Now what?" he said.

"We must carry on," said Emma. "*Someone* will see our sign soon."

"Let's move it to a better place," said Will.

But when they moved the sign, they saw exactly what was wrong. Someone had added two new words.

Windows cleaned by Will and Emma. NOT very cheap. NOT For charity.

They were changing the words
back again when Mr Petchy himself
came by and stopped to look.

"Do you do *big* windows, or
small windows?" he asked.

"Then here's two small windows for you." He took his glasses off and handed them to Emma.

A pair of glasses! That wasn't much of a job. All the same, Will dipped the glasses in a bucket and Emma rubbed them with a cloth. They came up sparkling.

"Good," said Mr Petchy.

"That's two pence for each
window. Four pence altogether."
Then they heard a horrible
hooting sound from over the road.
It was Trevor Tapp, laughing.

"Take no notice," Mr Petchy told them. "You did a good job so now you can clean some *big* windows. Come with me and I'll show you."

SPLENDIFLORA FANTASTICA

Mr Petchy marched them to a heavy door at the side of his house and took a large key from his pocket.

Will and Emma held their breath. Mr Petchy was going to take them into the back garden, a place where no one ever went!

The door creaked open. There in the distance were the windows Mr Petchy wanted them to clean. The biggest greenhouse they'd ever seen!

"There must be lots of plants in that," said Will.

"Come and see," Mr Petchy said. "Come and meet Flora."

He opened the greenhouse door but they could see no sign of Flora. All they saw was one huge flower pot with a single plant in it. A spindly, thin plant with a floppy stem and one weedy leaf.

"We had some like that," Emma said.

"Not like this. This is the Splendiflora Fantastica. The only one in the country," said Mr Petchy.

It didn't look like a Splendiflora Fantastica. It looked like a soggy drinking straw.

"Where's Flora?" Emma asked, looking round.

"This is Flora," said Mr Petchy and he pointed at the plant. "She won't flower, though. I've tried everything."

He waved his fingers at the plant. They *are* green, thought Will. But nothing happened.

Mr Petchy went indoors and left them to get on. In no time at all they were wiping and polishing the greenhouse glass, inside and out.

After a while, Will noticed that the hedge at the bottom of the garden was moving. It jiggled and trembled.

Sure enough, a big, brawny face was poking through the leaves. Then the face disappeared.

Will and Emma went down the
garden to see what Trevor Tapp
was up to.

On the other side of the hedge was a field. In the field were three quiet cows chewing the grass, and Trevor Tapp running about with a bucket and spade. Backwards and forwards he went, stopping here and there to shovel something into the bucket.

"What *is* he doing?" Will said.

"Collecting cowpats, I think," said Emma.

"Don't mind me," Trevor Tapp called to them. "I'm only having a bit of fun."

When his bucket was full, he stirred the mixture with his spade. Then he carried it over to the hedge. He began to swing the bucket.

"He's going to throw it!" said Will. "Quick! Do something!"

THE PERFECT MIXTURE

"One..."

"He'll spoil all our work!" Emma yelled.

"Two..."

They ran to the greenhouse, but what *could* they do? They couldn't move it. They couldn't cover it.

"THREE!" shouted Trevor Tapp.

A sloppy brown mess came flying over the hedge like a huge, dark rain-cloud. Straight for the greenhouse. Will jumped in the way and spread his arms. It was the only thing he could think of.

There was a slurping, smacking
sound and he disappeared beneath
the sloppy brown mess. And there
he stood – a brown snowman with
blinking eyes.

Trevor Tapp stuck his face
through the hedge and hooted.

"Look at him!" he chortled. "And
look at your sparkling windows!"

Half the greenhouse was covered
with muck. There were only two
clean patches. One was shaped
like Will with his arms spread out.
The other was the open door.

"Oh no!" cried Emma. "The Splendiflora Fantastica!"

She ran in to see if it was all right and...

Disaster.

A dollop of cowpat had landed in the flower pot. Another dollop dripped from the single, weedy leaf.

"We'll just have to clear up," said
Emma firmly, "and start again."

But there was no time to clear
up. Mr Petchy was striding down
the garden.

"What have you done to my lovely Flora?" he cried.

The garden was full of noise. Trevor Tapp laughing behind the hedge. Mr Petchy shouting. Birds screeching and cows mooing.

Then there was another sound.
A faint rustling.
"Listen," Emma said, holding up
her hand. "What's that?"

Mr Petchy stopped shouting and
listened. The birds and the cows
cocked their heads and listened, too.

The rustling was getting louder.
A thick green stem curled out of
the greenhouse. It twisted up the
side and climbed to the roof. As it
went, big leaves unfolded. Lush,
sprouting leaves as big as shirts on
a washing-line.

"It's the Splendiflora Fantastica,"
said Emma quietly. "It's growing."

More and more stems came out
of the greenhouse. One gripped a
garden fork and tossed it in the air.
Another twined round a
wheelbarrow and pushed it aside.

Along each stem were buds the size of coconuts. One of them burst open – POP! – and the strangest, most dazzling flower appeared.

"Oh Flora, my beauty!" said Mr Petchy with tears of joy in his eyes. "You're flowering at last!"

"It's magic," Will said in a whisper.

"It's cowpats!" said Emma.

"Cowpats!" cried Mr Petchy.
"I never thought of cowpats. Well done, well done!"

Magic isn't everything!

The birds watched with their beaks hanging open. Four astonished faces stared through the hedge – Trevor Tapp and the three cows. The cows seemed rather pleased with themselves.

POP! POP! More flowers burst open and Mr Petchy's garden was alive with colour and movement.

Then one of the stems twisted towards the hedge. It lifted itself and swayed from side to side. Trevor Tapp's head disappeared and he went running away across the field.

FLOWER POWER

People came from miles around to see the Splendiflora Fantastica at the Flower Show. There were cameras and microphones and reporters all over the place.

Everyone wanted to know about this wonderful new flower. And who was there to answer all their questions? Trevor Tapp, of course.

He stood in the middle of an excited crowd, boasting about how he had discovered the secret of the cowpats.

"It was all my doing," he said.

He didn't notice the thick green
stem creeping through the crowd
to curl round his ankle. He was
folding his arms to pose for a
picture when he felt a tug – and
down he went.

"Help!"

The Splendiflora Fantastica didn't
help. It dragged him backwards
across the lawn.

"Ow! Urgh!
Nn-neeuugh-EECH!"
And Trevor Tapp
was dangling by his
ankle in the
air. One
moment
he was
over the cake stall...
"WH-OA!"
...and the
next he
was upside-down
above the pond.
"WHO-OAH! Help!
Help! Get me down
from here!"

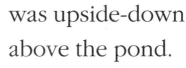

It was the highlight of the show –
a boy being swung through the air
by a plant. Cameras flashed and
people *oohed* and *aahed* with
wonder.

"You'd better let go, Flora, my
sweet," Mr Petchy said to his plant.
He wagged a green finger at it –
and the Splendiflora Fantastica
let go.

Down came Trevor with a slap and a slurp. Mr Petchy's pond was a muddy one, a soup of ooze. Slimy things were in that pond, and now Trevor Tapp was in there with them.

The crowd fell silent. Then a
sludgy head bobbed to the surface,
dripping with mud. The plant
opened and shut its flowers a little,
like someone winking.

"Don't mind Flora," Emma and
Will told Trevor Tapp. "She's only
having a bit of fun!"

More ~~SPRINTERS~~ for you to enjoy!

- *Little Stupendo Flies High* Jon Blake   0-7445-5970-7

- *Captain Abdul's Pirate School* Colin McNaughton 0-7445-5242-7

- *The Ghost in Annie's Room* Philippa Pearce   0-7445-5993-6

- *Molly and the Beanstalk* Pippa Goodhart   0-7445-5981-2

- *Taking the Cat's Way Home* Jan Mark   0-7445-8268-7

- *The Finger-eater* Dick King-Smith   0-7445-8269-5

- *Care of Henry* Anne Fine   0-7445-8270-9

- *The Impossible Parents Go Green* Brian Patten   0-7445-7881-7

- *Flora's Fantastic Revenge* Nick Warburton   0-7445-7898-1

- *Jolly Roger* Colin McNaughton   0-7445-8293-8

- *The Haunting of Pip Parker* Anne Fine   0-7445-8294-6

- *Tarquin the Wonder Horse* June Crebbin   0-7445-7882-5

All at £3.99

LITTLE STUPENDO FLIES HIGH

The return of the world's greatest double act – the Great Stupendo and his even greater daughter, Little Stupendo!

Jon Blake started writing for children during his brief career as a teacher. Since then he has had a number of jobs, from community centre warden to part-time lecturer. He is the author of several books for young people, including *The King of Rock and Roll* and *The Hell Hound of Hooley Street*, as well as the picture books *Impo* and *You're a Hero, Daley B!* He has written two other books about the famous Stupendos: *Little Stupendo*, which was shortlisted for the Children's Book Award, and *Little Stupendo Rides Again*. He has also written plays for television and the stage.

Books by the same author

Little Stupendo
Little Stupendo Rides Again
The Supreme Dream Machine

JON BLAKE

LITTLE STUPENDO

Illustrations by Martin Chatterton

TED SMART

First published 2001 by Walker Books Ltd
87 Vauxhall Walk, London SE11 5HJ

This edition produced 2002 for
The Book People Ltd, Hall Wood Avenue,
Haydock, St Helens WA11 9UL

2 4 6 8 10 9 7 5 3 1

Text © 2001 Jon Blake
Illustrations © 2001 Martin Chatterton

The right of Jon Blake to be identified as author
of this work has been asserted by him in accordance
with the Copyright, Designs and Patents Act 1988

This book has been typeset in Garamond

Printed and bound in Great Britain
by The Guernsey Press Co. Ltd

British Library Cataloguing in Publication Data:
a catalogue record for this book
is available from the British Library

ISBN 0-7445-5970-7

CONTENTS

CHAPTER ONE

Everyone needs a holiday. Even the world's greatest stunt artist. That's why Little Stupendo was sunning herself on the beach at Malibu, outside her Aunt Juno's beach hut.

"This is the life," said Little Stupendo. "I wonder what Dad's doing?"

This is what the Great Stupendo
was doing – banging his head on
the wall. Then he wrung his hands.
Then he stamped his feet.

"Why isn't she back yet?" he
cried. "I've got a stunt tomorrow,
and I need help!"

The Great Stupendo rang his old friend, Marvo the Memory Man, to see if he could help.

Marvo was famous for his fantastic memory act. The trouble was, Marvo was getting older. His memory wasn't what it used to be. In fact, it was next to useless.

"Hello," said Marvo,
"this is Albert Hall.
No, not Albert Hall.
Frank Tomato.
No, that's not right
either."
"Marvo?" said the
Great Stupendo. "This is
your old friend, the Great Stupendo."

"Ah, Great
Stupendo!" said
Marvo. "Who?"
The Great
Stupendo
wondered if
this was such
a good idea.

Next day, Marvo and the Great Stupendo dragged a mattress to the Market Square, where a crowd was gathering.

"Right," said the Great Stupendo. "You keep the crowd back, while I climb to the top of City Hall."

"Climb to the top of City Hall?" said Marvo. "Why?"

"So I can jump off it!" said the Great Stupendo, who was getting very impatient with Marvo.

"Jump off it," said Marvo. "Right, I see."

With that, the Great Stupendo put on his sticky-fly boots and climbed right up the side of City Hall. The crowd went quiet. The Great Stupendo prepared to jump.

Meanwhile, Marvo was looking at the mattress with a frown on his face.

"Who's dumped this in the square?" he grizzled.

Marvo took hold of the mattress and began to drag it away.

Just then, Marvo heard a loud noise behind him.

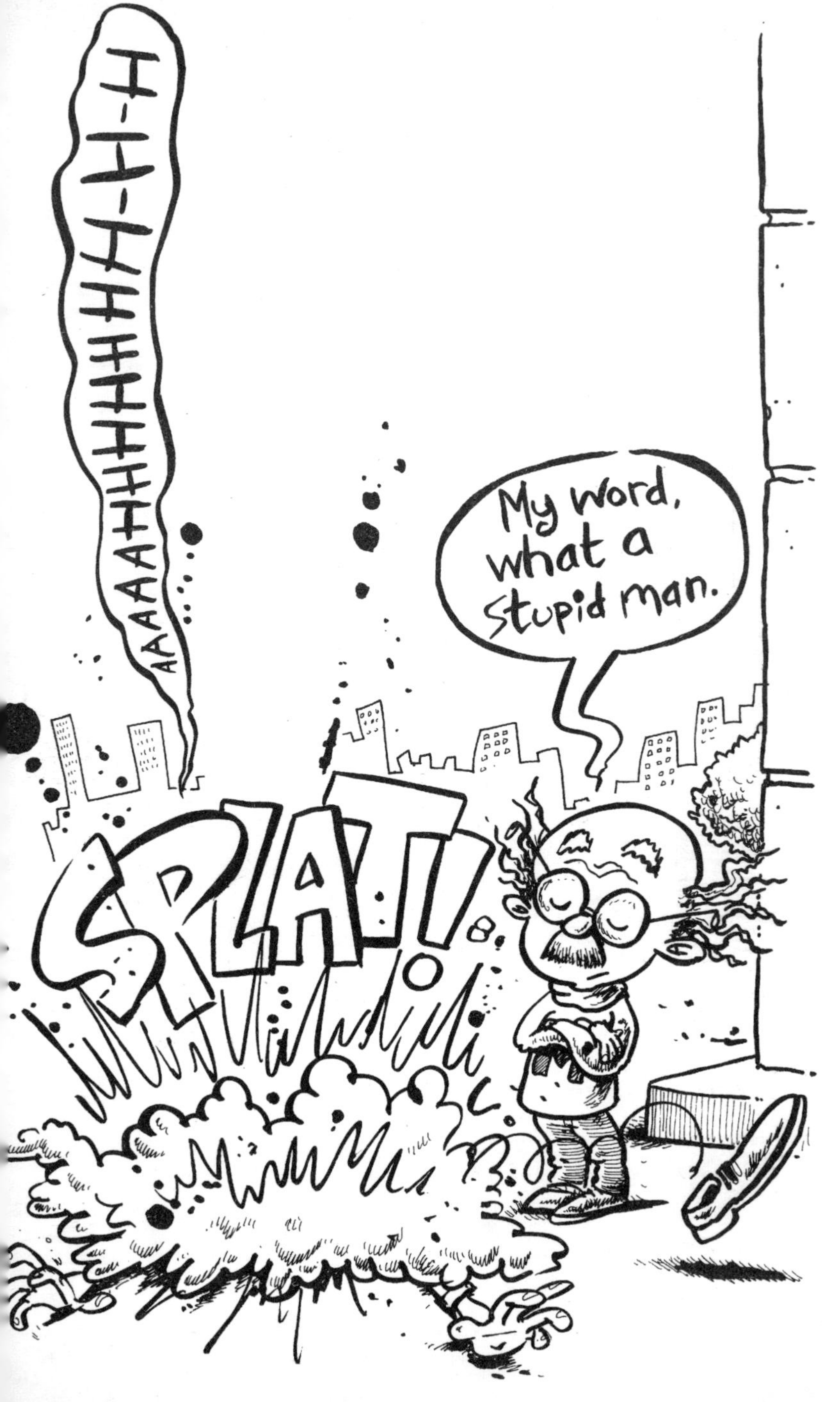
AAAAAAHHHHHHHHHHH-H-H-H
SPLAT!
My word, what a stupid man.

CHAPTER TWO

The Great Stupendo looked a sorry sight at the City Hospital. He couldn't do anything except make paper planes. He'd made about three hundred so far. The room was knee-deep in them.

"I'm so bored!" he moaned.

Just then the door opened, and in walked Little Stupendo. She was relaxed and tanned after her holiday with Aunt Juno.

"How are we going to do our act now?" said Little Stupendo.

"We aren't," croaked the Great Stupendo. "Not for ten weeks."

"Ten weeks!?" cried Little Stupendo. It seemed like a lifetime.

"You could always knit," replied the Great Stupendo.

Little Stupendo pulled a sick face. "How many times must I tell you?" she said. "I hate knitting! I want *action*!"

"But you can't do stunts on your own," said the Great Stupendo.

"Why not?" said Little Stupendo.

"Because," said the Great Stupendo.

"Because what?" asked Little Stupendo.

The Great Stupendo smiled, placed his big hand on her little hand, and put on a look of great wisdom. "Just because," he said.

Little Stupendo fumed. She *hated* it when he said that. It made her even more determined to prove she could do stunts on her own.

Little Stupendo began to imagine the new acts she could work on…

Little Stupendo began to feel miserable. None of her ideas were going to work. But just then, she reached into her pocket, and pulled out one of her dad's paper planes.

That's it! she thought to herself. *I'll do aeroplane stunts!*

Little Stupendo looked up
FLYING SCHOOLS in Phony Pages.
There was only one advert:

Little Stupendo didn't much like the sound of this flying school. But, as it was the only one, she decided to give it a go.

CHAPTER THREE

Soon, Little Stupendo found herself in a big, lumpy field, with nothing in it but a barn and a caravan.

Suddenly the caravan door burst open and there stood a sneaky-faced man in an old flying jacket. "Welcome!" he cried. "Give me all your money and I'll show you to the plane."

Little Stupendo did as she was asked, and Sid Honest led her to the big barn.

There inside was the oldest plane she had ever seen.

Little Stupendo climbed into the pilot's seat. Sid Honest handed her a flying helmet and a book called *How to Fly in One Quick Lesson.*

The noise of the engine drowned out Little Stupendo's words. The old plane started bumping crazily over the field, with the engine spluttering.

Little Stupendo flicked through
the pages of *How to Fly in One
Quick Lesson*. She twisted this, she
tweaked that, and she pulled on
the joystick with all her might. The
plane gave a little hop, then a
jump, then bumped back down. It
just wouldn't take off.

Meanwhile, in the field next door, the vicar of St Peter's was having a very nice tea party. Everybody sat about in their very best clothes, using the very best china.

Suddenly…

"That's it," said Little Stupendo. "I'm going to find a proper aeroplane."

Later that day, she arrived at Hugeville International Airport.

"Now these are *real* planes," she said to herself, watching the mighty monsters take to the skies.

Up ahead was a huge building with a sign saying WORLDWIDE SUPERJET INC.

Little Stupendo walked straight in and asked to see the manager.

"Can *I* be of assistance?" barked a loud, chilling voice.

A tall woman stood before Little Stupendo. Her suit had huge shoulders and her hair was like a crash-helmet. "I am Angela Power," she boomed. "Managing Director of Worldwide Superjet Inc."

"Can I fly one of your planes?"
asked Little Stupendo.

Angela Power laughed and
laughed, then patted Little
Stupendo on the head and laughed
some more.

Little Stupendo felt like giving up. But as she walked home, she remembered the conversation with her dad at the hospital:

Little Stupendo got angry all over again. She would show her dad, *and* that Angela Power!

Just then, Little Stupendo passed by Goosey Park. It was covered by a huge fair, full of lights and people and crazy rides. And there, right in the middle, was a machine called Virtual Flight.

Little Stupendo bought a ticket and got into the machine. To her delight, it was exactly like the cockpit of a big airliner.

In no time Little Stupendo was at
the controls, dipping the make-
believe wings, dropping the make-
believe wheels and landing on the
make-believe runway.

"This is brilliant!" cried
Little Stupendo. And she
ran all the way home
with her arms stretched
out like mighty wings.

But Little Stupendo wasn't finished yet. Oh no. Back home, she went straight for her piggy bank and filled her pockets with coins. Then she ran all the way back to the fair and paid for ninety-three goes on Virtual Flight.

The crowd had all gone home. The lights of the fair were all out. But Little Stupendo was still at the controls of her make-believe plane.

CHAPTER FOUR

Next day, Little Stupendo marched
straight into Angela Power's office.

"I am Little Stupendo," she said.
"I know how to fly and I want to
fly your plane."

This time Angela Power did not laugh. "You again!" she said. She reached for the button marked Security Guards. Then she thought again.

"Maybe I *could* use you," she said. Angela Power opened a cupboard and handed Little Stupendo a uniform. "Put this on," she said, "and report to the 10:30 flight to Addis Ababa."

Little Stupendo couldn't believe it. A pilot's uniform! She hurried to the toilets to try it on.

Little Stupendo was in for a nasty surprise. It wasn't a pilot's uniform at all. It was a flight attendant's uniform! Little Stupendo wouldn't be flying the plane – she'd be serving the tea!

At least I'll be on the plane, she thought.

The 10:30 to Addis Ababa took
to the sky. It was a massive great
plane, with hundreds of hungry
passengers. Little Stupendo did her
best to serve them, but she soon
got fed up. You couldn't do many
stunts when you were serving hot
coffee, or balancing trays of
Mississippi Mud Pie.

If only I could get in the pilot's cabin, she thought to herself.

But Little Stupendo couldn't even get *near* the pilot's cabin. She was run off her feet, all the way to Addis Ababa, *and* halfway back.

Then, out of the blue, Little
Stupendo got her chance. All the
passengers were asleep and the
other flight attendants were putting
their feet up. Little Stupendo crept
to the front of the plane and poked
her nose through the curtains. It
looked fantastic. The two pilots sat
at a great deck of controls, steering
the plane through the clouds like a
hot knife through butter.

Suddenly Captain Snow looked round. "Ah," he said. "Have you brought our hot milk?"

"A big dollop of syrup in mine, please," added Captain Sputnik.

Little Stupendo hurried back, fetched the captains' drinks and put them on the floor between them.

"Excuse me," she said, "but would you like another pilot?"

Captain Snow laughed. "Two is quite enough," he said.

"That's right," added Captain Sputnik. "If anything happens to Captain Snow, I can fly the plane, and if anything happens to me, Captain Snow can fly it."

"So nothing can go wrong," said Captain Snow.

With that, Captain Snow and Captain Sputnik both dived for their hot milk.

There was no time to lose. Little Stupendo seized the controls of the plane. At last!

She picked up the intercom:

"Ladies and gentlemen," she said. "This is your new captain speaking. I hope you are enjoying your flight. Please fasten your seatbelts as I will now be trying a few stunts."

With that, Little Stupendo took the plane straight up like a rocket …

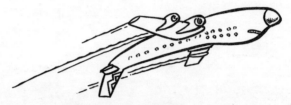

flew upside down …

dipped the wings …

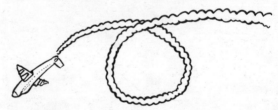

and looped the loop.

WARNING TO CHILDREN:
ALWAYS ASK PERMISSION FROM AN ADULT
BEFORE FLYING AN AIRLINER.

"This is madness!" cried Hester
Prune from Tunbridge Wells.

"This is fun!" squealed her seven
children.

Little Stupendo was having the time of her life. But there was a nasty surprise in store for her. A red warning light began to flash on the control panel.

"The fuel tank!" she gasped.

The plane was still miles from the airport. There was only one thing for it. Little Stupendo had to make an emergency landing.

Little Stupendo turned the plane and began to bring it down. It was then she saw the sign:

CITY HOSPITAL

That was where she was!

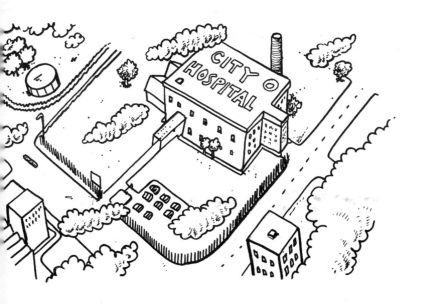

Meanwhile, the Great Stupendo was folding his nine-thousandth paper plane. As he looked out of the window, his eyes nearly popped out of his head.

Little Stupendo waggled her
wings, and lowered her wheels,
and aimed the aeroplane like a
dart. All her hours of practice were
paying off. Smooth as silk, she
touched down and taxied down
the make-do runway.

All over the hospital, doctors were
dropping their pens, and patients
were rushing to the windows.

"Wh-who's that at the controls?"
asked the Great Stupendo.

The Great Stupendo gawked as
the huge airliner came closer …

closer …

closer …

"Little Stupendo!" gasped the
Great Stupendo.

The great plane eased to a halt. Little Stupendo waved to the crowd that had gathered below. Then she slid down the escape chute and did a double-tuck somersault onto the ground. There was a huge cheer.

The Great Stupendo wheeled his way through the crowd, still in his pyjamas.

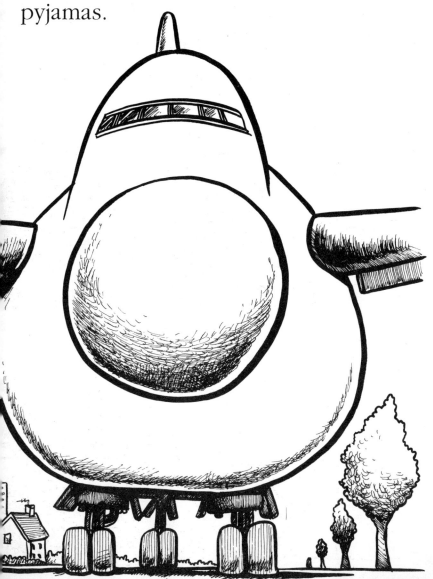

"Little Stupendo!" he said. "You … you flew *that*!"

Little Stupendo nodded happily and patted the aeroplane's giant wheel.

"Better than knitting, eh, Dad?"

More *SPRINTERS* for you to enjoy!

- *Little Stupendo Flies High* Jon Blake   0-7445-5970-7

- *Captain Abdul's Pirate School* Colin McNaughton 0-7445-5242-7

- *The Ghost in Annie's Room* Philippa Pearce   0-7445-5993-6

- *Molly and the Beanstalk* Pippa Goodhart   0-7445-5981-2

- *Taking the Cat's Way Home* Jan Mark   0-7445-8268-7

- *The Finger-eater* Dick King-Smith   0-7445-8269-5

- *Care of Henry* Anne Fine   0-7445-8270-9

- *The Impossible Parents Go Green* Brian Patten   0-7445-7881-7

- *Flora's Fantastic Revenge* Nick Warburton   0-7445-7898-1

- *Jolly Roger* Colin McNaughton   0-7445-8293-8

- *The Haunting of Pip Parker* Anne Fine   0-7445-8294-6

- *Tarquin the Wonder Horse* June Crebbin   0-7445-7882-5

All at £3.99

TAKING THE CAT'S WAY HOME

"Jan Mark has created another superb novel for early readers… This thoughtful story may give some children inspiration and hope in dealing with bullies." *The School Librarian*

Jan Mark is one of the most acclaimed authors of books for young people. She has twice been awarded the Carnegie Medal and has also won the Penguin Guardian Award, the Observer Teenage Fiction Prize and the Angel Award for Fiction. Her many titles include *Thunder and Lightnings, They Do Things Differently There* (shortlisted for the 1994 Whitbread Children's Novel Award) and *Lady Longlegs.*

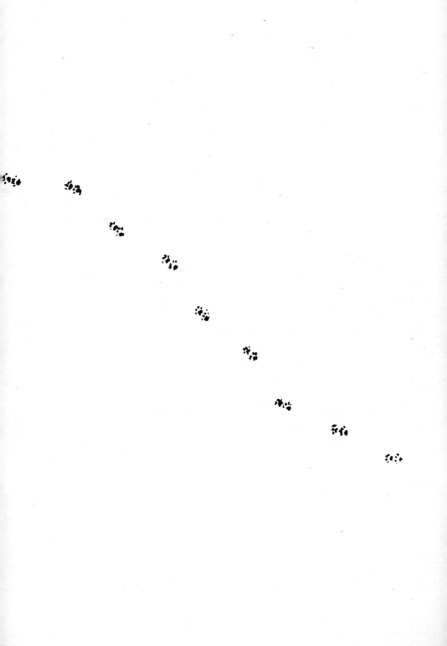

Books by the same author

Lady Long-legs
The Snow Maze

For older readers

The Lady with Iron Bones

JAN MARK

Taking The Cat's Way Home

Illustrations by Paul Howard

TED SMART

For Hamid and Nafeesa
J.M.

For Ted and Eric
P.H.

First published 1994 by Walker Books Ltd
87 Vauxhall Walk, London SE11 5HJ

This edition produced 2002 for
The Book People Ltd, Hall Wood Avenue,
Haydock, St Helens WA11 9UL

2 4 6 8 10 9 7 5 3 1

Text © 1994 Jan Mark
Illustrations © 1994, 2001 Paul Howard

The right of Jan Mark to be identified as author of this
work has been asserted by her in accordance with the
Copyright, Designs and Patents Act 1988

This book has been typeset in Sabon

Printed and bound in Great Britain by The Guernsey Press Co. Ltd

British Library Cataloguing in Publication Data:
a catalogue record for this book is
available from the British Library

ISBN 0-7445-8268-7

Contents

Chapter One

Jane's cat was called Furlong.
People said, "What a strange name
for a cat," until they saw him. Then
they understood. Furlong had a face
and a tail, two ears and four feet.
The rest was fur. You could hardly
see his legs.

Kind people said, "What a fine cat." Rude people said, "That's not a cat, it's a feather duster."

William, at school, said, "That's not a cat, it's a loo brush," but that was not the worst thing he did.

Andrea never said things like that, because she liked Jane and she loved Furlong. Andrea lived next door. She was one year older than Jane, so they were not in the same class at school, but they were friends.

10

"I can remember when you were born," Andrea said to Jane. This was not true, but she said it sometimes so that Jane would remember that Andrea was much older. Jane could not say that she remembered when Andrea was born. Even Furlong was older than Jane.

Every day Jane and Andrea walked to school together, on their own, because there were no roads to cross and lots of other people were going to school as well.

Jane's mother said to her, "Don't step in the road. Don't talk to strangers. Never let anyone give you a lift." She said it every day as Jane went down the path.

Then Andrea came out of her
house and they walked together
along the street, every day. Every
day, Furlong went with them.

First of all he ran in front, and
when he got to the corner he sat
and waited for them. When they
turned the corner, he ran to catch
them up and walked beside them.

When they turned the last corner,
Furlong ran on ahead and sat by the
school gate until they got there too.
Jane and Andrea stroked him and
said goodbye.

Then they went in to school and
Furlong walked home by himself.
Jane thought he walked back the
way they had come, but he did not.
He had his own way home.

Everyone knew Furlong, all the people in Jane's class and all the people in Andrea's class. The teachers knew Furlong. So did Mrs Giles, the caretaker, and the lollipop lady. Mrs Kumari, the school secretary, knew Furlong because one wet morning he put his muddy paws on her new pink skirt. Jane was afraid she would be cross, but Furlong smiled in his fur and purred, and Mrs Kumari forgave him.

Everyone knew Furlong except William.

William was new.

Chapter Two

One morning Jane and Andrea were saying goodbye to Furlong when a new dad and a new boy came along the street.

"What a fine cat," the new dad said. This was the proper thing to say to Furlong, but the boy just glared.

Jane looked at the boy and the boy looked at Jane. He put out his tongue and made his eyes go funny.

When Jane went into her classroom the new boy was there with Mr Singh. Jane liked Mr Singh because he was kind and he had lovely whiskers, like Furlong.

"This is William," Mr Singh said.
"He is going to be in our class. Who
has an empty space at their table?"

Jane sat with Matthew and Habib
and Alison. There were two empty
spaces at their table. "Don't put up
your hand," Jane said to Alison.

18

She remembered the face that
William had made when he saw
Furlong. "We don't want him here."

But Matthew and Habib put up
their hands and jumped up and
down, so Mr Singh sent William to
sit on one of the empty chairs.

He sat down opposite Jane and made his eyes go funny again. Then he kicked her, under the table.

At break time William went off with Matthew and Habib and they all stood together under a tree and whispered.

When it was time to go in again, Jane looked at William's chair and said to Alison, "Will you change places with me?"

"No, I won't," Alison said. "I don't want him making funny eyes at me."

When everyone had come indoors, Mr Singh said, "Now, get out your News books."

He gave William a book to write his News in.

William wrote, "My name is William."

He looked at Jane. Then he wrote, "I do not like cats," and turned his book round so that Jane could see what he had written.

Jane wrote, "There is a new boy at our table. He does not like cats. I do not like him."

Habib leaned over and said, "Why don't you find another table to sit at?"

"Yes," said Matthew. "We don't want any girls on this table, do we?"

They had never said anything like that before.

Chapter Three

Next morning Jane said to Mum, "I don't want to go to school today."

"Do you feel poorly?" Mum asked.

"There's a new boy at school," Jane said. "He doesn't like cats."

"Lots of people don't like cats," Mum said. "You will have to get used to that."

"He doesn't like me, either," Jane said, but she still had to go to school.

She walked down the road with Andrea and Furlong. Furlong ran ahead, and sat and waited, and walked behind, and then overtook them and ran to the school, just as he always did.

People stopped and said hello to Furlong, and Furlong purred and waved his feathery tail.

Then William came along, without his dad. He did not say hello to Furlong. He leaned down and said "Sssss!" very loudly, and Furlong jumped away. No one had ever said that to him before, not even Mrs Kumari when he put mud on her skirt.

William said "Sssss!" again, and
Furlong was frightened. He jumped
on to the wall of the house by the
school and his fur stood on end
because he was angry.

"Leave my cat alone," Jane said.

Andrea said, "If you do that again I'll tell Mr Singh, and he will make you stand in the corridor."

"That's not a cat," said William. "That is a loo brush."
Then he picked up a stone and threw it.

The stone did not hit Furlong but it scared him. He jumped on to the top of the wall and ran away, under the trees.

"I hate you!" Jane shouted, and
hit William. William hit Jane, and
Andrea ran inside to fetch Mr Singh.

"I can't have you fighting," Mr
Singh said when he came out.

"She hit me first," William yelled.

"He threw a stone at Furlong,"
said Jane.

"Go inside at once," Mr Singh
said. He was angry. Even his
whiskers looked angry.

28

When they got to the classroom he
said, "William, you are not to throw
stones at *anything*. Go and sit down."
William sat down and kicked Alison
under the table.

"Now, Jane, stop crying," said Mr
Singh. "You ought not to have hit
William, even if he did throw a stone."

"But Furlong was frightened," Jane
said. "He ran away. He'll get lost."

"I don't suppose he will," Mr Singh said. "He's a grown-up cat and he knows his way about. Which way did he run?"

"He went along the wall by the school field," Jane said.

"Well, then, he was going the right way," said Mr Singh. "You live in Kemp Street, don't you? Cats have their own way of getting around. They don't have to walk in the street, like us."

Jane went to her table.

"Tell-tale. Tell-tale," William hissed.

"Tell-tale," said Matthew and Habib.

"I'll get you tonight," William said. "After school, I'll get you."

After school William's dad came to meet him.

"I'll get you tomorrow, then," said William.

Jane and Andrea ran all the way home and when they got there Furlong was sitting in the garden, washing his toes. Mr Singh was right. Cats have their own way home.

Chapter Four

When Andrea and Jane and Furlong walked to school next day, William was waiting at the gate.

As soon as Furlong saw William, he jumped on to the wall. William did not even have time to say "Sssss!"

"Loo brush!"
William shouted
instead. Furlong
turned round
and ran away
along the wall
beside the
school field.

"I don't care," Jane
said loudly. "Cats have their own
way home."

"Tell-tale," William said. "I'll get
you after school."

"I'll get you after school," William
said, at break.

"I'll get you after school," William
said, at lunch time.

33

"William's going to get you at home time," said Matthew and Habib at afternoon break.

At home time Mr Singh told them to go. William went out quickly with Matthew and Habib, to lie in wait for Jane.

Jane stood at the gate with Andrea. William's dad was not there today,

but they could see William's head poking round the corner, at the end of the road. When William saw Jane and Andrea, he hid.

"He's going to get us," Jane said.

"No he isn't," Andrea said. "We won't go home that way. We'll go home the way Furlong goes."

She climbed on to the wall of the
house by the school. It went up like
steps until it was as high
as the wall by the
school field.

"Quickly," Andrea said. "Here
comes William."

Jane climbed on to the wall,
walked up the steps and followed
Andrea.

William and Matthew and Habib
were already running down the street.
· Andrea began to run and Jane
ran behind her, along the wall. Then
they stopped.

"Did they see us?" Andrea said.

"Where are you?" William shouted, in the street.

They could not see him and he could not see them.

"I can see you!" William yelled.

"He can't," Andrea said. "He thinks we're hiding by the gate. Come on."

"It's a long way to the ground," Jane said.

"Don't look down," Andrea said.
"Walk slowly. We need not hurry
now. Pretend you are walking on a
tightrope."

Jane did not think that this would
help.

"I know where you are! I'll get
you," William shouted, far away.

Jane thought how silly he must
look, and she felt better.

Chapter Five

On one side of the wall was the school field. Mrs Giles was pushing a machine up and down, making white lines on the grass for sports day. She did not see Andrea and Jane.

On the other side of the wall was a row of back gardens. They passed a garden full of roses and a garden full of rubbish. Things looked different from the top of the wall. This is what birds see, thought Jane. This is what Furlong sees.

Next they came to a garden with an apple tree at the end of it. Jane knew that tree. It hung over the field and in autumn people picked up the apples that fell from it.

Now the apples were small and green, Jane and Andrea had to step carefully over the branches.

Then they met a white cat sitting on the wall. It would not move. They had to step over the cat, too.

In the next garden was a prickly
bush. It scratched their legs and
Jane was afraid that they would fall
into it, but they got past the prickly
bush. In the garden after that, two
people were sitting in deckchairs.
One of them turned round and
shouted, "Oi! What are
you doing up there?
Get down at once!"

"Run!" said
Andrea, and they
ran for seven
whole gardens,
over branches and
through prickly
bushes, along the wall.

43

At last they came to the end of
the school field.

"We must turn left here," Andrea
said. Now they were on the wall
that ran along the end of the
school field. There were no trees
in these gardens and they could
walk quickly.

Then Jane said, "Look."

Mrs Giles was not in the field
any more, but over by the school
was William. Matthew and Habib
had got bored and gone home, but
William began to run. Far away
William shouted, "Now I'm going
to get you!"

"He's seen us," Andrea said.
"Quick. When we get to the next
garden, turn right. There's a big tree
to hide in."

It was a very big tree with very big
leaves. It stood in a corner and four
walls met under it, like a crossroads.

"This way," Andrea said, and they
ran along a wide wall, out of the tree.

"Turn left," Andrea said. "Turn right. Turn right again."

They stopped running and looked round. They could not see the tree, or the school field, but they could see William.

Now William was on the wall as well, but he was going the wrong way.

They stood quite still until he was out of sight. He was still shouting, "I can see you!"

"We're safe," said Andrea.

"We're lost," said Jane.

Chapter Six

They stared all round. Jane was
right. The gardens looked different
from the top of the wall, but the
houses all looked the same.

"Our house has a window in the
roof," Andrea said.

"My house has a creeper growing up it," Jane said.

They looked and looked, but most of the houses had windows in their roofs, and a lot had creeper growing up them. They sat on the wall and wondered what to do.

"Let's go back," Jane said, but they could still hear William shouting far away, and they did not know how to go back.

"Mum will be waiting. She'll be cross," Jane said, and she began to cry.

"Don't be a baby," Andrea said, but she knew that her mum would be worried too if they did not get home soon.

"There is a swing in our garden," Jane said, and they looked again. There were five gardens with swings in them.

"We've got a shed," said Andrea.
All the gardens had sheds.

"I wish we could find a
policeman," Andrea said, but there
were no policemen walking on the
walls, only cats.

Jane watched the cats and then
she had an idea. She stood up and
shouted, "Furlong! Furlong!"

"Don't be silly," Andrea said.

"It's not silly," Jane said. "I have a
special voice for Furlong. He always
comes when I call." She shouted
again. "Furlong! Furlong!"

They waited, and waited.

Nothing happened.

"Try once
more," Andrea
said, and Jane
called again.
"Furlong!
Furlong!"
Then Andrea
stood up
and pointed.
"I see him."

Far away a ginger cat was running along the wall towards them, waving his feathery tail. He came closer and closer. It was Furlong.

He ran up to Jane and put his muddy paws on her skirt. Jane stroked him. "Good Furlong," she said. "Now, take us home."

Furlong knew
the way. He ran
along the wall
and then sat
down and waited for
them to catch up with him.
He turned left and
they followed
him. He turned
right and they ran

behind. He jumped on to the roof
of a shed at the end of the garden.

There was a swing
in the garden and
a creeper was
growing up the
side of the house.

The house next door had a window in the roof.

Jane's mum was taking the washing off the line. When she saw Jane and Andrea on the wall she dropped all the washing.

"Where did you come from?" she said, and ran to help them climb down.

"We've been taking the cat's way home," Jane said.

Then they heard William's voice again, but William was not shouting now. Far away, William was running along the wall, and William was crying.

William called, "Mum! Mum! I'm lost! Dad, I'm lost!" William had no cat to show him the way home.

"Who is this?" said Jane's mum when William reached Jane's garden.

"It's a poor little boy who has got lost," Andrea said, loudly.

Jane's mum lifted William down
from the wall and led him indoors.

"Tell me where you live,"
Jane's mum said, "and I will take
you home."

She walked down the street with William and made him hold her hand.

Jane and Andrea stood at the gate and watched. They did not say anything, but they smiled.

And Furlong, in his long fur,

smiled too.

More *SPRINTERS* for you to enjoy!

- *Little Stupendo Flies High* Jon Blake   0-7445-5970-7
- *Captain Abdul's Pirate School* Colin McNaughton 0-7445-5242-7
- *The Ghost in Annie's Room* Philippa Pearce   0-7445-5993-6
- *Molly and the Beanstalk* Pippa Goodhart   0-7445-5981-2
- *Taking the Cat's Way Home* Jan Mark   0-7445-8268-7
- *The Finger-eater* Dick King-Smith   0-7445-8269-5
- *Care of Henry* Anne Fine   0-7445-8270-9
- *The Impossible Parents Go Green* Brian Patten   0-7445-7881-7
- *Flora's Fantastic Revenge* Nick Warburton   0-7445-7898-1
- *Jolly Roger* Colin McNaughton   0-7445-8293-8
- *The Haunting of Pip Parker* Anne Fine   0-7445-8294-6
- *Tarquin the Wonder Horse* June Crebbin   0-7445-7882-5

All at £3.99

THE FINGER-EATER

Long ago, in the cold lands of the North, there lived a troll named Ulf, who had a very bad habit – he liked to eat fingers!

Dick King-Smith used to be a farmer and is now one of the world's favourite children's book authors. Winner of the Guardian Fiction Award for *The Sheep-pig* (filmed as *Babe*), he was named Children's Book Author of the Year in 1991 and won the 1995 Children's Book Award for *Harriet's Hare*. His titles for Walker include *Puppy Love*, *Dick King-Smith's Animal Friends*, *Lady Lollipop* and the popular Sophie series.

Books by the same author

Lady Lollipop
Sophie Hits Six
Sophie in the Saddle
Sophie Is Seven
Sophie's Lucky
Sophie's Snail
Sophie's Tom

DICK KING-SMITH

THE
FINGER
EATER

Illustrations by Arthur Robins

TED SMART

For Gareth
A.R.

First published 1992 by
Walker Books Ltd, 87 Vauxhall Walk
London SE11 5HJ

This edition produced 2002 for
The Book People Ltd, Hall Wood Avenue,
Haydock, St Helens WA11 9UL

2 4 6 8 10 9 7 5 3 1

Text © 1992 Fox Busters Ltd
Illustrations © 1992, 2001 Arthur Robins

The right of Dick King-Smith to be identified as author of this
work has been asserted by him in accordance with the
Copyright, Designs and Patents Act 1988

This book has been typeset in Garamond

Printed and bound in Great Britain by The Guernsey Press Co. Ltd

British Library Cataloguing in Publication Data:
a catalogue record for this book is
available from the British Library

ISBN 0-7445-8269-5

CONTENTS

CHAPTER 1

Long long ago, in the cold lands
of the North, there lived a most
unusual troll.

Like all the hill-folk (so called because they usually made their homes in holes in the hills) he was hump-backed and bow-legged, with a frog-face and bat-ears and razor-sharp teeth.

But he grew up (though, like all other trolls, not very tall) with an extremely bad habit –

he liked to eat fingers!

11

Ulf (for that was his name) always went about this in the same way.

Whenever he spied someone walking alone on the hills, he would come up, smiling broadly, and hold out a hand, and say politely:

"How do you do?"

Now trolls are usually rude and
extremely grumpy and don't care
how anyone does, so the person
would be pleasantly surprised at
meeting such a jolly one, and
would hold out his or her
hand to shake Ulf's.

Then Ulf would take it and, quick
as a flash, bite off a finger with his
razor-sharp teeth and run away as
fast as his bow-legs would carry
him, chewing like mad and grinning
all over his frog-face.

Strangers visiting those parts were amazed to see how many men, women and children were lacking a finger on their right hands, especially children, because their fingers were more tender and much sought after by Ulf.

Nobody lacked more than one finger, because even small children weren't foolish enough to shake hands if they met Ulf a second time, but ran away with them deep in their pockets.

It was usually the index finger that Ulf nipped off because it was the easiest to get at, so that many children grew up pointing with a middle finger…

and holding a pencil between middle and third…

but sometimes Ulf went for the little one: thumbs, for some reason, he did not seem to fancy.

Strangely, the people of those lands were tolerant and long-suffering and seemed to put up with Ulf's bad habit.

"What can't be cured must be endured," they would say, and since they considered it was no use crying over spilt milk, they wasted no tears over lost fingers but got on with their lives with only seven.

CHAPTER 2

Who knows how long Ulf the troll
might have continued in his wicked
ways if it had not been for a little
girl named Gudrun.

Gudrun was the only child of a reindeer farmer. She had golden hair which she wore in a long plait, and eyes the colour of cornflowers.

Indeed she was as pretty as a picture, looking as though reindeer butter wouldn't melt in her mouth.

She was also a sensible child, who paid attention to what her parents told her.

One evening, as they all sat round the fire outside their tent, Gudrun's mother said to her:

Remember, you must never shake hands with a troll.

She stirred the cooking-pot that was suspended above the flames. The hand that held the ladle had no little finger.

With his right hand, on which the index finger was missing, Gudrun's father picked up a stick to put on the fire.

25

"But why," said Gudrun, "didn't either of you do that?"

"When we were both children," said her mother, "we didn't know about the Finger-eater."

"We were among the first in this district," said her father, "to lose a finger. But now everybody knows."

"Why don't all the mothers and fathers warn their children then?" said Gudrun.

"They do," said her mother, "but sometimes the children don't listen, or they just forget. Mind you remember."

Gudrun thought deeply about
this while she was out on the hills,
helping her father herd his reindeer
as they grazed their way across
the slopes.

It's all very well, she thought, to tell children not to get their fingers eaten, but someone ought to tell that troll not to eat them. Eating people's fingers is wrong.

And being not only a very pretty
but also a very resolute child, she
resolved that she would stop the
Finger-eater. But how?

"Father," she said as she sat
milking one of the reindeer,
"how big is a troll?"

"No taller than you, Gudrun," her father said, "but much much stronger."

"Have you ever met one?"

For answer her father held up
his right hand.

"Oh yes," said Gudrun. "But since then, I mean?"

"No," said her father, "but I have quite often seen the hill-folk, just for

a moment. Then they scuttle down their holes, for they are all shy of people. Except Ulf the Finger-eater."

"You have never seen him again?"
"No, and nor will you, I hope."
But not long after, Gudrun did.

CHAPTER 3

Even in those bleak Northern lands
there are days in the short summer
which are bright and warm and
flower-filled, and on such a morning

Gudrun's father handed her a flask.
It was made of reindeer skin, was
this flask, and it was stopped with a
cork made out of reindeer
horn, and it was
filled with fresh,
rich reindeer
milk.

"Be a good girl and take this to your mother," her father said, for the herd's grazing grounds were not far from the family tent, and it did not occur to him that she might come to any harm.

Gudrun set off across the hill,
carrying the flask in her right hand.
Before she had gone far she saw,
in a steep bank, a large hole.

Could that be the home of one of
the hill-folk? she thought, and no
sooner had she thought it than out
of the hole came a hump-backed,
bow-legged figure with a frog-face
and bat-ears.

Straight towards her he came, his mouth agape in a friendly smile, his hand outstretched. "How do you do?" he said politely.

The Finger-eater! thought Gudrun
and she remembered her parents'
advice to put her hands in her
pockets and run. But I won't, she
said to herself bravely, for now may
be my only chance to make the
Finger-eater see how wrong it is to
eat fingers. So she stood her ground.

"I'm sorry," she said, "but I cannot shake your hand because I'm holding this flask of milk."

"You could always hold it with your other hand," said Ulf, for it was he.

"I could," said Gudrun, "but I won't. I've heard of you, you see. You are Ulf the Finger-eater."

"Well, well," said Ulf, passing his tongue across his razor-sharp teeth, "and what is your name, little girl?"

"It's Gudrun. Now let me tell you something, Ulf," she said. "Eating fingers is wrong."

A clever little miss, thought Ulf. How can I trick her? He sat down on a nearby tree-stump, and crossed one bow-leg over the other, looking serious and thoughtful.

"You're right, Gudrun," he said. "I'm wrong to eat people's fingers, I see that now. But at least give me a drink of milk."

And when she holds out the flask, he thought, I'll soon have one of those lovely little pink sausages!

"Not on your life," said Gudrun. "Thanks to you, both my mother and my father are short of a finger."

"How time flies!" said Ulf. "That must have been when I was a very young troll. I've probably had a hundred fingers since then."

"Well, you're not having a hundred and one," said Gudrun, "but on second thoughts I'll give you that drink," and pulling out the cork, she jerked the flask so that the milk shot out straight into Ulf's frog-face, and as he stood gasping, she dashed away.

Chapter 4

Gudrun did not tell her parents
of her meeting with Ulf. She simply
said she had tripped, the cork had
come out of the flask, and the milk
had all spilled (a white lie, she
told herself).

But she continued to think long
and hard about the Finger-eater.
Somehow or other he must be
made to give up his horrid habit.

Then one day Gudrun had a
sudden, brilliant idea.

She was sitting outside the family
tent, playing with a reindeer antler.
This was the time of year when all
the reindeer (for the cows are
horned as well as the bulls) shed
their antlers before growing fresh

ones, and they were lying about
everywhere. Hard as iron they
were, and many of them were of
the strangest shapes, for reindeer
antlers are very large and many-
pointed, those of some of the
bulls curving right round
and down until they
almost meet the
animals' faces.

The single antler that Gudrun
held was quite a small one, probably
from a young beast, but at its tip it
had an odd shape, something like
a human hand. It had at its end a
flat surface resembling the palm of
a hand and from this surface five
points protruded.
Just like four
fingers and
a thumb,
thought
Gudrun,
and that was
when the
idea hit her.

That afternoon Ulf emerged from his hole to see Gudrun approaching, her long blonde plait swinging as she walked, her cornflower-blue eyes sparkling, her right hand, much to the troll's surprise, already outstretched in greeting. Admittedly she was wearing a large pair of reindeer hide gloves, but those won't save her, thought Ulf.

He advanced to meet her.

"Hello, Ulf," said Gudrun brightly.
"I've come to say I'm sorry for
throwing the milk at you. Will you
shake hands and then we can be
friends?"

Stupid child, thought Ulf. She's
asking for it. This time I won't just
have one finger, I'll have all four,
and he grabbed Gudrun's right hand
and shoved it into his frog-mouth
and bit it as hard as he could.

Then Ulf's great cry of agony echoed and rang from the circling hills, as his razor-sharp teeth broke and smashed and shattered, every one.

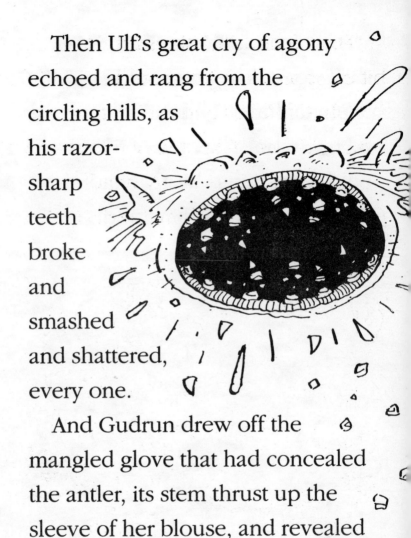

And Gudrun drew off the mangled glove that had concealed the antler, its stem thrust up the sleeve of her blouse, and revealed that bony five-pointed end that had looked so like a hand.

"Hard luck, Ulf," she said. "You bit off more than you could chew."

"Oh! Oh!" moaned the Finger-eater. "My teeth! My teeth! Every single one is loose in my head! Oh, it is agony! Help me! Help me!"

"I will," said Gudrun, and she
took from the pocket of her skirt a
pair of stout pliers, a useful tool
with which her father was wont to
draw stones that had lodged deep
between the great splay hooves of
his reindeer.

"Open wide, Ulf," she said, "and
I'll make you a much better troll."

Then with the pliers she pulled
out the teeth of the Finger-eater,
one by one, till none were left.

CHAPTER 5

Even after that, Ulf could not
easily rid himself of his bad habit.

Once his mouth was no longer sore, he still tried several times to live up to his name, but thanks to Gudrun, he could not. For though the reindeer can grow new antlers, hill-folk cannot grow new teeth, and those few people whose hands he caught only giggled at the harmless pressure of his toothless gums upon their fingers and told him not to be such a silly old troll.

So that before long Ulf fell into a
terrible sulk, and disappeared down
his hole in the hill, and was never
seen again.

And even today, if you travel in the cold old North and stay amongst the reindeer people, you may hear the tale of the troll named Ulf and the girl called Gudrun, and how she and she alone put paid to the wicked ways of the Finger-eater.

More SPRINTERS for you to enjoy!

- *Little Stupendo Flies High* Jon Blake   0-7445-5970-7

- *Captain Abdul's Pirate School* Colin McNaughton 0-7445-5242-7

- *The Ghost in Annie's Room* Philippa Pearce   0-7445-5993-6

- *Molly and the Beanstalk* Pippa Goodhart   0-7445-5981-2

- *Taking the Cat's Way Home* Jan Mark   0-7445-8268-7

- *The Finger-eater* Dick King-Smith   0-7445-8269-5

- *Care of Henry* Anne Fine   0-7445-8270-9

- *The Impossible Parents Go Green* Brian Patten   0-7445-7881-7

- *Flora's Fantastic Revenge* Nick Warburton   0-7445-7898-1

- *Jolly Roger* Colin McNaughton   0-7445-8293-8

- *The Haunting of Pip Parker* Anne Fine   0-7445-8294-6

- *Tarquin the Wonder Horse* June Crebbin   0-7445-7882-5

All at £3.99